SECOND WIND

Short Stories

TERRY F. TORREY

Visit terryftorrey.com for a complete list of works by Terry F. Torrey, and subscribe to the newsletter to be notified of promotions, special events, and new releases of things worth reading.

This is a work of fiction. All of the characters, organizations, and events portrayed in this work are ether products of the author's imagination or are used fictitiously.

2024-01-09

Dedicated to Elizabeth.
I'll always be your biggest fan,
and work to make you mine.

CONTENTS

STRANGE DAYS

STORM TREES

As the clouds darkened and swirled above, the forest below came alive. Excitement bristled at the edge of the woods, then rustled all throughout. The trees came out of a stupor, shaking their branches and glittering their leaves in anxiety and alarm.

A storm is coming!

On a little knoll, the tallest tree in a stand of mighty sycamores watched the lightning crackle from cloud to cloud and began to creak and groan, overcome with worry.

Down by the brook, a weeping willow tried to end it all. With a baleful cry, it lifted its branches to the flicking tongues of electricity above, begging to be taken.

In the end, a mighty spruce tree felt the fury of the lightning. A jagged bolt reached down from the sky and touched its crown. Its trunk exploded, and its roots sizzled in the ground. Its branches gave a mighty sigh, and the air filled with the scent of pine.

And then it was over. The storm passed. The clouds lifted and the lightning danced away, leaving the trees to dry themselves in a gentle summer breeze.

THE RED BALLOON

None of us saw where it came from. Jimmy was the first to see it. He was only about four, and he didn't know the words to really say it right, but we all heard him yelp in that excited and happy kind of way, and when we turned around, there it was: a red balloon, swirling on the breeze coming out of the alley beside the hardware store, rising slowly in the summer air. It wasn't anything special, just a dirty red balloon tied with a long, thin, pink ribbon. Suddenly, though, we all wanted it. All of us.

Jimmy reached out both sticky hands to it as it drifted slowly past his head, but he was too uncoordinated and clumsy, and he missed it even though it went right past his head and even dragged the ribbon up over his shoulder.

From the alley, it rode the little breeze out toward the street. Jimmy's sister, Elaine, ran to grab it. She was a couple years older than Jimmy, wearing a sundress and the composure of a little girl. She thought she had it, but it twitched on a puff of wind, up over old man Johnson's car, just out of reach of her fingers.

Tommy had been crossing the street, coming back from the

Dairy Queen to flaunt his ice cream cone in front of the rest of us. He was nine and we all hated him. When the red balloon popped up over the car and into the street, it was almost in his face. He was startled to find it so close at hand, and though he made a desperate grab, dropping his ice cream cone in the process, he missed it. It hovered for a moment over his head, agonizingly just out of reach, before leaving him, rising to the middle of the street.

"I'll get it," said Ralph. He was older than the rest of us, and he'd just come out of Newton's barber shop. He quickly pulled the slingshot out of his back pocket, dropped to one knee, and picked up a pebble out of the gutter by the curb. He pulled the pocket of the slingshot way back and held it. His left eye closed and his tongue stuck out a bit as he took careful aim, then there was a brisk *thwish*. We all gasped as the red balloon danced sideways, and the pebble flashed under it.

Now the balloon had risen as high as the windows of the apartment over the laundromat across the street, and the breeze carried it up and across the street from us. Jimmy began to sob. "It's getting away!" cried Elaine. Tommy's hands flew to his face in horror. Even Ralph had turned frantic, desperately locating another pebble, then pulling the pocket of his slingshot back so far that one of the rubber bands broke.

Then a shadow swept over us. We didn't have to turn to recognize the deep, reassuring voice of Sheriff Gordon. "Don't worry there, children," he said. "I'll get that balloon for you." And we knew that he would.

We heard him unsnap his holster as he took out his service weapon, but none of us flinched or covered our ears. By now the balloon had risen as high as the clock on the front of the bank, looking as small as the head of a push pin, and growing smaller by the moment.

The sound of the gunshot echoed back and forth across the

street, and we all wanted to cheer. We watched the balloon anxiously. The pink thread of ribbon seemed to quiver, but the red balloon did not fall.

Sheriff Gordon fired again.

We never found out where the red balloon came from, and we were never able to explain to anyone why it affected us so much. None of us were ever the same after that day when the red balloon came into our lives, then drifted away. We could never forget the image of Sheriff Gordon, his left arm bent and bracing his right at the elbow, firing shot after shot over our heads, up at the red balloon, until he ran out of bullets and the balloon was just a distant speck, and then just a memory.

Years later, Elaine would still burst into tears at the mention of it. Tommy developed a nervous tic. Little Jimmy began to stutter, and Ralph never picked up a slingshot again.

Sheriff Gordon took it hardest of all. They found him back behind the transformer station, dead in his squad car. He'd filled it with red balloons, climbed into it with them, and put a bullet through every last one of them.

They say he saved the last bullet for himself.

SPINNER

He was eight years old, and they called him Spinner, because nobody had ever seen anybody that could spin a quarter like he could.

Then one day at a diner in Knoxville, where the countertop was polished to a fine sheen, they set him up on a vinyl stool seat and asked him to show off his stuff. He was happy to oblige.

He held the quarter on edge under his left index finger, wound up the same finger on the other hand, and gave the coin a mighty flick. Off went the coin in a whirling blur with a whine like a jet engine. The overhead lights flashed off the gleaming silver onto his smiling face.

People held their breath. It spun, and it kept on spinning.

He was eight years, four months, and twenty-one days old: 3063 revolutions of the Earth. The quarter spun at twenty revolutions a second, and it kept spinning for two minutes and thirty-three seconds, ultimately reaching 3063 revolutions.

And at that precise instant, with a great gasp from the crowd, both Spinner and the quarter fell over, and spun no more.

PEACE OF MIND

That morning, the fat man rose uncharacteristically early. He shaved his face clean and dressed in his cleanest suit: dark blue slacks, a white shirt, a blue tie with thin diagonal yellow stripes, and a gray sport coat. He put some certificates and some business cards into his brown briefcase, then set out for the day. His station wagon coughed up and down the dusty country roads, stopping at little homes here and there in the hills.

He had no luck at all.

Four doors were slammed in his face. Three people kicked him out before he even finished his pitch. Two people smiled and said they had no money. And one person threatened to get his gun.

Then he stopped at a dirty yellow trailer in the back of a shaded park. The trailer smelled like dry rot and old smoke, but he didn't mind. He got through his spiel, he wasn't picking up any bad signs, and it was time to go for the close.

"So then," he said, "all I need to get you started is three hundred dollars. That will cover the hundred-dollar application fee, and two hundred for your first annual premium."

He sat back in the kitchen chair and smiled, running his fingers over the space where a smudge of a goatee might have been.

The little old woman sitting across the table turned to her husband and put her wrinkled hand on his. "Two hundred dollars a year," she said hungrily. "That other man on the phone told us it would be more than that every month."

The little old man chewed on his unlit pipe. "Yup," he said. He was staring hard at the paper in the center of the table, but his face showed the strain of the calculations going on in his head. He reached into the pocket of his plaid shirt, took out the plastic pouch of pipe tobacco, and turned it over and over in his hands. He rocked his upper body a little. "That's about twenty dollars a month, isn't it?"

The fat man's face flickered and his eyes flashed up to the ceiling for just a moment. Then he smiled, showing a mouthful of little yellow teeth more picket than fence. "Yes, sir, I believe you're right."

The little old man gave a satisfied grunt.

"Ooh, that's such a small amount for life insurance, we'd be foolish not to, don't you think?" the woman asked of her husband.

"Yup," he said.

"And you'll finally have peace of mind," the fat man said, his curved sausage link of a smile punctuating his pauses. "Won't it be a tremendous burden off your hearts to know that you finally have life insurance?"

"It sure will," said the woman, and her milky eyes shone. "I think I should get the money. I think we should do it." She turned to the fat man. "Can you take cash?"

The fat man's smile grew wider, showing a large tongue. "Cash? Yes, that would be wonderful."

The little old woman scooted her chair back across the

linoleum, went to the cupboard over the counter by the white refrigerator, and took down a rusty-bottomed coffee can.

The little old man opened the package of tobacco and tamped a wad into the bowl of his pipe.

The fat man watched the little old woman empty most of the small bills out of the can. He licked his lips as she brought them over and counted out three hundred onto the table.

The husband struck a match and held the flame to the bowl of the pipe. His eyes turned down to the money on the table as he puffed the pipe to life. The scent of vanilla rum filled the small kitchen.

The little old woman put her hand on the stack of bills and looked at the little old man's face.

"Yup," he said, without looking up, with a nod.

The little old woman slid the money over to the fat man. He folded the bills and put them in his jacket pocket.

"Aren't you going to count them?"

"Naw," he said. "I've always found folks of your generation to have the highest principles. It's the younger people you have to watch out for."

The little old woman beamed tremendously at this.

"Yup," said the little old man.

The fat man turned to the floor beside his chair, clicked open his briefcase, and brought up a paper that said *Certificate of Insurance* in large, ornate letters. He stuck a sharp black pen in his left fist. His brow furrowed and his tongue peeked out of the corner of his mouth as he carefully lettered the names of the little old couple.

When he was finished, he handed the trophy over. "You're going to want to put that with your other important papers."

The old woman, still beaming, held the paper at arm's length to look at it. She nodded to herself. "I sure will," she said.

The fat man spread his fingers on the edge of the table and

pushed his chair back. "Well, then," he said. "I believe it's time for me to let you good folks get back to your happy retirement."

The little old woman leaped to her feet. "Oh, do come back soon," she said. "We get so few visitors out here, and it's wonderful having a nice young man stop to see us."

"All right, ma'am," said the fat man. "I'll see you again real soon. Y'all take care now."

"Yup."

In the months that followed, the little old couple kept the certificate in a shoe box in their closet, tucked safely away from the jealous eyes of their friends, the suspicious eyes of their neighbors, and the angry eyes of their daughter. Everyone spoke badly about the new insurance, one way or another, but few could deny that the little old couple seemed to glow with new life. Their steps had a new spring, and their eyes had a new twinkle.

No one in these parts saw the fat man again for the rest of the year, but one fellow said he saw someone that looked like him at a rehab clinic a couple towns down the interstate. The little old couple paid no mind to that.

The following spring, to the amazement of the neighbors, the fat man's station wagon turned in to the circular driveway of the trailer park and gasped to a stop in front of the dirty yellow trailer. The fat man pulled himself out of the car, plopped a green derby onto his head, and went up to the screen door. His hand shook a little as he knocked.

He was welcomed at once into the kitchen with its familiar scent of vanilla rum smoke.

The little old woman got the coffee can down and counted out three hundred dollars onto the table.

The fat man held up a hand. "Gone up this year," he said, his eyes shining over the pads of his cheekbones. "Comp'ny raised all the premiums twenty dollars."

"It's worth it," said the little old woman. "It's given us such peace of mind, as good as the Lord."

"Peace of mind," the fat man repeated. He nodded, thinking. "That's what I sell."

"Yup," said the little old man.

NO GOOD DEED GOES
UNPUNISHED

I sat in jail two days, long enough for my public defender to explain the long list of charges against me, before the mayor called me into his office. He wore a dark suit and a red tie. The chief of police wore mirrored sunglasses and had his thumbs hooked into his belt. I wore an orange jumpsuit and a frown.

The mayor picked a list up from his desk. "Breaking and entering. Unlawful city use of city property." He looked up at me. "Grand theft."

I glanced uncertainly from face to face. "I didn't *steal* them," I said. "I *replaced* them."

"I don't know," said the chief of police. "The charges look pretty solid to me."

The public defender had said the same thing. I swallowed hard and said nothing.

"I'm not sure prison is the right place for you, though," the mayor said. "Maybe I could arrange for some special community service."

"What kind of community service?"

"Some of the equipment down at police headquarters is getting pretty old." He looked up with a twisted smile. "It could stand to be ... replaced."

THE DESERT'S REVENGE

The old lady yelled *help* in such a funny voice he could hardly keep from laughing. He pushed her down the hall of her trailer and pressed a pillow over her face until she quit kicking him. He was so strong, he could hold the pillow with one hand!

On his way out, he took the keys to the 1970 Monte Carlo off the hook in the kitchen. He filled the tank with cash from the old lady's purse and headed east. He drove the scenic route, watched his mirrors, and minded the speed limit all the way across the border into Arizona.

Forty miles down a bad road, he realized he must have missed a turn, and he was headed into the empty desert. That's when he heard a *POP* and felt the steering wheel jerk.

Five minutes later, he assessed his situation grimly. The spare had rotted to the rim, the temperature soared past one hundred ten, he had no water, and he hadn't seen another car in hours.

He had a choice: walk and die on the road, or stay and die in the car.

Either way, the desert would take the old lady's revenge.

SUSPICIOUS BEHAVIOR

o save this message, press one. To delete this message, press two...
 beep
Message has been deleted. To undelete this message, press one. To double-delete this message, press two...

Huh?

beep

Message has been double-deleted. To undelete this message, press one. To super-double-delete this message, press two...

...

"Hi, I got a voicemail message earlier tonight, and I tried to delete it, and your system wouldn't let me."

"Did you try pressing two?"

"Yes. Lots of times, but it doesn't *get rid* of the message, it still keeps it, so I can get it back any time, and I don't want to get it back. I just want it deleted."

...

"Hi, Bob, it's Steve over in Customer Service. I got a call from a customer freaking out about our delete system." A pause. "Yep. System says he pressed two more than ten times before calling us. What is that? Quantum-extra-super-double-delete?" Chuckles. "Yeah, I've already forwarded the message to you. You're definitely going to want to find out what *this* guy's hiding."

MISS DIRECTION

It looked like an elaborate dance, but at root it was a simple sleight of hand.

They walked the streets in their black robes, and those who did not ignore them were happy to see them. They shared their prayers with a desperate people in a blighted city.

But sometimes, as they passed a bank, one of them would find something, perhaps a bit of trash to be picked up off the sidewalk. Behind this misdirection, there would be a faint swish of robes, and one of them had simply disappeared.

Inside the bank, the workers' eyes went wide as they became the latest victims of the daring robber who appeared and vanished wearing nothing but a gun belt.

A minute later, when the robber disappeared, no one again noticed the rustle of robes.

Yes, it was a simple magic trick, but it worked every time. After all, who would ever suspect a kindly group of nuns of bank robbery, especially when they stopped to share prayers for all who asked, and the black of their robes was one of the bright spots of the dirty city?

AMERICAN MADE

We made widgets, darn good widgets, and I was proud to make them. I sanded the edges carefully, smoothed out all the bumps, painted and polished each piece. These widgets would find their way to customers who wanted—expected—the best, and I was proud to make them.

My co-worker, Harold, wasn't so proud. Frequently I'd catch him sending pieces along with burrs on the edges. Sometimes I'd notice that he'd skipped the second coat of paint.

"Harold," I'd ask, "how can you send that piece along like that?"

"What difference does it make to you?"

"Well, none, I suppose, but don't you have any pride in your work?"

He'd laugh. "You sure are a character."

We had rates, production goals we were supposed to meet. We were supposed to make X number of widgets every hour. I worked quickly, diligently, trying my best to send out widgets that were worthy of pride. I had a hard time meeting the rates. My hands ached from the work.

Harold never had a problem meeting the rates, even though he went outside to smoke a lot.

One day, the boss—the big boss—called me into his office.

"Is there some problem down on the floor?" he demanded.

I nodded wisely. I had known this would come. "Yes," I admitted, sad that it would be me to have to break the news. "I didn't want to be the one to say anything, but I've seen him sending widgets through with burrs, and sometimes skipping the second coat—"

"I don't want to know about that," he barked, cutting me off. "I want to know about you. Why aren't you meeting your rates?"

"Uh," I said, surprised. "I, I just try to make sure the widgets are right before I send them along." I swallowed hard. "I just want them to be right."

"What? They don't have to be perfect, just send them along. I'm selling this place, and if you aren't meeting your rates, the buyers don't want to pay so much."

"But the widgets—"

"Fuck the widgets! I don't care about them, I care about the money. Now get down there and meet those rates. Don't make me call you up here again."

"Yes, sir," I said. I looked down and watched my feet leaving his office.

When I got back to my station, Harold tried not to smirk.

RENDEZVOUS

On a beach in a quiet tropical cove, Frank Caldwell took off his sandals and walked barefoot. With every step, the sand between his toes began to melt the giant block of stress inside his chest. Here, again, was paradise.

On a volcanic island many miles away, a section of hillside broke free and slid down into the water, shoving a wave of tremendous energy out across the sea.

On the beach, Frank Caldwell sat down and leaned back against his hands. He closed his eyes and listened to gulls he had not seen.

In the open ocean, the massive wave barely registered as a ripple in the water.

On the beach, Frank Caldwell gazed quietly out at the world for the last time. The sunshine embraced him in warm serenity.

When the wave came up onto the beach, it was so strong as to be incredible, and so swift as to be inescapable. As it took him, Frank Caldwell was not overcome with fear, or despair, but merely the thought: what a long way we've both come to meet our end here together.

Then Frank, and the wave, were gone.

HEROES

Outside, in the parking lot of the Empire Hotel, Virginia Shuler sat in her Honda Civic, breathing deeply, seemingly on the verge of hyperventilating. The bright lights of the parking lot reflected brilliantly off the rivulets of rain tracing down her windshield. She took no notice. Gradually, she got control of her breathing. Tipping her head back, she gazed at some unknown point beyond the white roof of her car. Focusing. Praying for strength.

Presently, she pulled herself together to her mission. She opened her purse, checking that the letters were still tucked inside. Satisfied and resigned, she picked the clipboard and the package up off the passenger seat, took one final deep breath, opened her door, and stepped out into the rain.

Upstairs and across the complex in room 273, Chandra Morelock had dropped her gym bag, picked up the phone, and dialed it. Now she stood with the receiver pressed to her ear, waiting anxiously for an answer. In her right hand, she held a newly opened letter.

"Jim Keller," said the voice on the line.

"Jim, it's Chandra."

"Chandra, hey—"

"I got another letter, Jim," she interrupted fervently.

"Calm down, Chandra."

"I can't calm down, Jim. This is getting really bizarre."

"Tell me about the letter."

Chandra sighed and tried to get a grip on herself. She continued pacing back and forth across the small room. "It says 'stay away from my daughter,' just like the last one."

"That doesn't sound like a serious cause for alarm."

"But then it goes on ranting to say that this is the 'final warning.'"

Jim was silent for a moment. "That's something different," he said finally.

"Damn right it is. It's very different, and very creepy."

"You know, you can pull out of the tournament if you want to. You don't have to win every championship. Maybe you can let someone else win a tennis trophy this weekend."

"I've never pulled out of a tournament in my life."

"Well, maybe it will be rained out. Didn't I see on the news that it's raining there?"

"It's not going to be rained out, Jim. This is Phoenix. Nothing ever gets rained out here."

"Well ..."

"Well, what, Jim? You're my manager. You're supposed to manage things like this so I don't have to deal with them."

"Well, what would you like to do? You can call the police if you really feel the threat is urgent."

Chandra paused and sighed heavily. "No, I don't really know what I'd tell them at this point," she said.

"Just tell them the truth," Jim volunteered. "Tell them you received a letter—"

"It's more than one letter," Chandra interrupted. "First it was a couple letters from some teenage fan, that I returned with those generic fan mail responses."

"Right."

"Then I started getting letters from someone claiming to be the mother of this fan, telling me to stay away from her daughter."

There was a pause on the other end of the phone. Finally, Jim said hesitantly, "and you only sent the form fan letters to the daughter?"

"Damn it, Jim, of course that's all I sent! I don't need you making accusations, too!"

"I'm just making sure I have the points clear here," Jim said soothingly. "So after this ordinary fan mail, you started receiving threatening letters from the girl's mother, right?"

"Yeah. I've received three letters from the mother. In them, the mother keeps making references to other letters she says I sent, saying I better stop trying to take her daughter away."

"Hmm," said Jim. "Any idea where she might have gotten these letters she keeps referring to?"

"No, no idea at all."

"Hmm," said Jim. "And now this 'final warning'?"

"Right. And the worst part is the address the fan gave, and the postmark of these letters."

"Which is probably what I think it is," said Jim, rather glumly.

"Phoenix," Chandra said, matching his glum. "Where I am for the tournament this weekend."

Downstairs in the lobby, Brian Hauser looked up from his post behind the front desk as a middle-aged woman walked in. Cradled in her right arm, she carried a long white box adorned with a pink bow and spotted by the rain. In her left hand, she carried a wooden clipboard with a few papers on it. As she approached the front desk, she looked down nervously at the clipboard.

"I need the room for Chandra Morelock, please," said the woman, a touch of nervousness in her voice.

"Excuse me?" said Craig.

"I have a delivery for Chandra Morelock," the woman repeated, glancing down at the white box. "I need you to give me her room number."

Craig was clearly distressed by this. "We're not allowed to give out room numbers," he said. "You can leave the package here, and I'll turn on her message light—"

"No, that won't do at all," the woman replied quickly. "These flowers won't keep. I need to deliver them right away."

Craig squirmed a bit inside his uniform tie. "You see, ma'am, it's just that we're not allowed to give out room numbers to anyone ..."

"We've all got our instructions, Brian," said Virginia, reading his name off the tag on his button-down shirt, gaining confidence. She glanced and nodded at the white paper on her clipboard. "My instructions say I'm to personally deliver these roses to Chandra Morelock."

Craig gave up. It would be all right just this one time, he supposed. "It's two seventy-three," he said. "Upstairs in the back."

Almost before he finished the words, Virginia was through the interior door, headed to the back of the complex.

Upstairs, Chandra continued her conversation with her manager. "What do you think I should do, Jim?"

"Well, I think the first thing you should do is to alert the hotel security, let them know what's going on."

"There *isn't* any security here that I know of, Jim."

"No security?"

"No. You have me set in this fleabag hotel for some kind of promotional thing. It isn't close to the tournament site, and there isn't any security here that I can tell."

"Perhaps," Jim said thoughtfully, "you should call the police."

"I don't have time to deal with them, Jim," Chandra argued. "My first match is early tomorrow, if it isn't rained out, and I don't have time to go into all the details with them." She paused thoughtfully. "Besides, what do I really have to tell them? What could they really do for me?"

"How about if I get a private security guard over there, then? A bodyguard to stand right outside your door for the night. Would that make you feel better?"

Chandra thought about this. "An armed guard," she said finally, "and I want him to go to the tournament with me tomorrow, too."

"All right, then, that's what we'll do. I'll make the arrangements from here, and in the meantime, you just get some rest."

"I don't think I'll be able to relax until he gets here, Jim."

"Well, I'll take care of everything, Chandra. I expect to have personal security there within an hour."

"Okay, Jim."

Downstairs, Virginia located the building containing rooms 164 through 289. The glass entry door was not locked. A smell of dust hit her as she entered the quiet building. To her left, an open door led to a staircase. There seemed to be no elevator. Her sturdy legs labored to carry her stocky frame upstairs. She was breathing heavily when she reached the second floor.

Here Virginia plodded solemnly past the ascending room numbers. The muffled sound of a television drifted under the first door she passed, but the rest of the rooms seemed unoccupied. In the middle of the hall, she stopped in front of the brown door of 273. She could see a sliver of light extending from under the door.

Her hands shook as she adjusted the purse under her arm and straightened the red bow on the long white box. With a final deep sigh, she reached a hand out and knocked lightly on the door. "Delivery," she announced almost quietly, her voice quavering slightly.

༺ༀ༻

Inside, Chandra was confused. She'd just hung up the phone with Jim Keller; surely the guard couldn't be there already. She wasn't expecting anyone else. Could this be her worst fear—coming true?

She jumped as another knock broke the silence. This time she heard a voice announce, "Delivery!"

This almost made her feel better. Almost. She wasn't expecting a delivery, but it wasn't entirely unusual for people to send her gifts. She tiptoed over to the door and peeked through the peephole. In the soft yellow light of the hallway, she could see a middle-aged woman holding a long white box with a bow on it.

Someone, evidently, had sent her some roses.

She opened the door. The woman outside seemed flustered, out of breath. "Chandra Morelock?" she asked.

"Yes," said Chandra.

"I have a delivery for you."

"I see."

"I'll need you to sign for it," the woman announced, offering forward the clipboard.

Chandra took the clipboard from the woman, then waited expectantly. "Do you have a pen?" she asked.

"Uh," said the woman. "No."

That was strange. "Oh," said Chandra. "I'll just get the one off the dresser." She turned back into the room, fetched the pen, and went to sign. "I don't see a delivery slip here," she said. "Where do I sign?" As she turned back to the woman, she heard a rustling.

The woman's face had been transformed into a mask of determination. In her hands she held a rifle as the box fell away from it to the floor.

Chandra's reactions, honed by years of tennis, took over immediately. In one athletic move, she ducked to her left and swept her right arm up backhand, catching the barrel of the rifle and pushing it upward. Continuing the move, she pulled the barrel forward over her.

As the rifle ripped from the woman's hands, the trigger caught on her finger and a shot blasted from the barrel and ripped into the ceiling.

Chandra's concentration was unbroken, and she pulled the rifle to her own control. As she brought it in to her body, the woman threw herself at Chandra. Bringing the rifle around, she easily brushed the woman aside. The woman fell heavily to the floor, her purse bouncing free and scattering letters over the carpet at the foot of the bed.

The woman spun around on the floor to find the rifle pointed at her face.

"Shoot me," she said.

"What?" Chandra asked.

"Shoot me," said the woman again.

"Who are you?" demanded Chandra.

"Shoot me," pleaded the woman. "You have to shoot me."

"What are you talking about?"

"I want you to shoot me." The woman was almost in tears now.

"What? Why?"

"Because I want my daughter back!"

"What?"

The woman was sobbing now. "I want my daughter back," she said plaintively. "You have to shoot me."

Chandra looked at the rifle in her hands, then pointed the barrel to the floor. "I'm not going to shoot you, crazy woman." Looking down at the letters on the floor, something caught her eye. "That's my name on the return address," she said.

The woman said nothing, still sobbing.

"I didn't send these letters," Chandra said. "Where did you get these?"

The woman still sat on the floor, only sobbing.

"Tell me where you got these letters!" Chandra shouted.

"I wrote them," the woman replied.

"You," said Chandra. "You're the one who's been sending me the letters, aren't you?"

The woman nodded.

Chandra looked at the letters on the floor again. Most of them had her name, but no address, listed in the return address space. "Why?"

"Because you stole my daughter!"

"What? I did no such thing."

"Yes, you did, you really did."

"How?"

"When she was a little girl, I was her hero. She wanted to be just like me and spend all her time with me. Then you came along."

"What are you talking about? I've never seen you or your daughter before."

The woman shook her head. "Not literally. You started playing tennis on TV, and she started watching you."

"So?"

"So suddenly she didn't want to be like me anymore. She wanted to be like you. You're a beautiful, rich athlete, and I bounce from one office job to another. How can I ever compete with you? When she started sending you fan mail, that's when I saw my chance."

This made no sense to Chandra. "So you came here to shoot me? How is that going to help you?"

"I didn't come here to shoot you. I came here for you to shoot me."

"Why would I shoot you?"

"For trying to keep you away from my daughter!"

Slowly the whole crazy scheme started to make sense to Chandra. "You poor, stupid, crazy woman," she said. "You set the whole thing up."

The woman was silent.

"You wrote letters that you pretended were from me, then wrote me letters from yourself to threaten me away from your daughter. Right?"

The woman nodded glumly.

"And you came here to confront me, knowing that I would take the rifle from you."

"And you're supposed to kill me. That way my daughter will see that I've given my life to protect her, and I'll be her hero again. Not you."

"What a charming little plan," Chandra replied sarcastically.

They were both silent for a few moments. Finally, Chandra went over and picked up the telephone.

"What are you doing?" asked the woman.

"Calling the police."

"You can't do that yet," complained the woman.

"Don't worry," replied Chandra. "You can still be her hero. But instead of being the hero who died defending her, you can be the hero who came up with a crazy plan to win her back."

"Do you think that will really work?" the woman asked, suddenly hopeful.

"It will have to do."

NERVOUS NIGHTS

ENLIGHTENED NIHILISM

"In the end," the young philosopher asked his mentor, "would you say there is hope for humanity?"

As the old philosopher opened his mouth to answer, he spotted a young woman moving down the sidewalk toward them in bouncy steps. She wore a bright yellow jacket and carried a black umbrella angled across her shoulder, and she glowed through the mist like a promise.

Suddenly, in her, he could see all the hope of humanity, all the dreams and ambitions, every plot and plan.

As she passed the bar, his gaze came to his own reflection in the window: beard going gray in ragged streaks, hair grown wild, black eyes sunken beneath a wrinkled brow. He flinched at the visage, and tequila shook from the glass over his fingers.

The young woman passed without a glance, and the yellow of her jacket receded quickly into the rainy evening, slipping away like the memory of a dream, a testament to wasted youth.

"Professor?" the young philosopher asked. "Do you—"

"No." The old philosopher gritted his teeth. "No hope at all."

CYCLE

Talking, talking, talking. What the *hell* is that noise?

I wake up frowning, frowning and blinking at the infomercial on the television. It's late. The rest of the room is dark. I feel—funny. I try not to recognize what it is, but I can't.

Shit. I've been drinking again. Hard. I feel light-headed. I'm probably still drunk. The room seems foggy and unstable. The clock on the wall says twenty after two. My mouth is dry. My joints are stiff. My limbs feel stiff and cold. My head is cloudy. Two-twenty in the morning.

I get up and turn off the television. I start to turn away—then turn back, staring. Was it on when I woke up, or was I only dreaming that it was on? Suddenly, I can't remember. I look at it, and I can't seem to make my eyes focus on it. Pinpoints of images seem to be pricking through the surface of the television. I catch glimpses of different shows. It's off, though. How can that be?

It doesn't matter. I'm drunk again, and I don't remember how I got here, how I got into bed. I hope I haven't done anything too embarrassing this time. I've been through this before. I know the drill. I'll need to keep a low profile until I get sobered up, and I'll need to keep away from people until I've put a few good nights between me and last night. First, though, I have to get things back in order, back where they should be, like nothing happened.

Shit.

Light from somewhere—the kitchen, the bathroom, I'm not sure I want to know—dimly illuminates the room, and I see that my jacket is not on the back of my chair. How drunk was I that I didn't put my jacket where I always put it?

I'm standing by the door, dressed now. Funny. Did I get dressed, or was I sleeping in my clothes? I don't remember waking up with my boots on. I look at my feet. The boots are there. Was I wearing them in bed? I look at the bed. It's made now. Was I sleeping on top of it? I thought I was in it. It looks ... funny to me. Made and unmade at the same time. And I don't remember getting that comforter.

I shake my head. It doesn't matter. What I really want to know is if I parked my motorcycle acceptably outside. I hope I didn't just lay it down in the driveway, or in the yard.

Suddenly I notice I'm wearing the jacket. What the fuck is going on here? I'm sure I wasn't wearing it when I woke up. Was I using it as a blanket, or a pillow? Did I put it on when I first stood up? That must be it.

I go to the door and look outside. My head is suddenly, inexplicably, filled with prayers—desperate, passionate, pleading prayers—that my motorcycle will be outside, in the parking lot where it belongs. For a moment this shakes me. The voice in my head, screaming and begging in prayer, is mine.

The motorcycle is not in the parking lot.

I'm out the door and most of the way down the sidewalk to

the parking lot before I even realize what I'm doing, and then I don't delay for even a step. There isn't anything to think about; there's only one thing to do: I've been drinking, and I got too drunk to drive home. I've left my motorcycle at the bar, which is not very far from my apartment. I've got to go get it. I'm not as drunk as I was before. I still feel woozy, but I know I can ride. I've got to go and get my motorcycle and bring it back here. Everything will be back to normal then. Everything will be back in its place, and this knot of fear will untie from the bottom of my esophagus.

I'm outside now, walking quickly toward the bar, and things aren't any better. The sidewalk feels unsteady under my feet. I can see the wind bending back the branches of the trees by the sidewalk and by the road, but I can't hear it blowing, and I can feel only the slightest puff of breeze on the right side of my face. I don't think about it. My head is really dizzy. I just want this night to be over.

I don't see any cars on the road. The sky has grown lighter, or something. It isn't exactly lighter the way the sky gets lighter, it's more of an exact shade of gray that it never gets, not even during a solar eclipse.

I try to avoid this by looking down at my feet, but the sudden movement causes the sky, the horizon, the road, the buildings—causes them all to shudder-shake, to vibrate and thrum and snap into place. I see them blur and refocus. I see the moon flip through cycles in the sky. When I blink I see a streak of a car flash past me on the road, sunlight glinting full of its windshield. I see all this and I know it's crazy, it's wrong.

And I remember a saying once that, when you think all the world's gone crazy, chances are it's only you.

I'm almost there. The bar I go to—my favorite bar—is only about a mile from my apartment. That's why it's my favorite bar. Driving home, it's just one quick right turn onto this road from the side street where the bar is, then one quick left turn into the parking lot of my apartment complex. Quick, and easy. I can do it drunk. I *have* done it drunk. Lots of times.

Approaching the corner, I am almost to the point where I'll be able to see the bar around the corner on the left when something catches my eye—off the road, to the right.

I stop dead in my tracks.

Something is there, at the base of a huge tree set back off the road. I don't want to look at it, and yet—my vision pans around to it involuntarily. My body turns to face it.

There's a form crumpled on the ground in front of the tree. A wrinkled fabric, shiny black like leather. I can see a riding boot. A little ways past it in the darkness I can see a piece of powder-coated steel, a bit of a frame lying on the ground, a shiny piece of chrome tailpipe sticking up.

No.

My head fills with shouts again. Desperate wailing pleas screaming in the night. Someone is praying—begging for another chance. My heart stops in my chest. It sounds like my voice.

No. It can't be—

I won't look at it. I *don't* look at it, and it can't be. It *won't* be.

I turned up the street, back toward home. My feet clattered on the sidewalk. My head seemed so light it felt as though it would explode. I was limping. I could feel something liquid on my leg, and I didn't dare look at it. And suddenly my left arm was numb.

The sky overhead shudder-shook, everything blurry then snapping back into focus. Some kind of gray streak slashed the blackness in half. Or was it blue? I didn't know. I didn't even want to know. I didn't want to think about it—about any of it. I just wanted to go home.

That's all I thought about. I just kept moving my feet and heading home. The ground washed over in crimson gray and I steadfastly ignored it. I had to get home, get to sleep. Everything would be all right if I could just make it home, get to bed.

The apartment complex was dark. The cars in the driveway didn't look right—didn't look familiar. It seemed to me that it had been light when I had left, just a few minutes earlier. I didn't want to look around, but I did. I could see the trees billowing in a strong wind, but I couldn't hear the air moving through the leaves or feel it on my face. It was as if I were walking in a bubble. Strange patches of sunlight flickered here and there on the buildings and the trees, almost as though a schizophrenic police helicopter were shining a spotlight around the complex.

I didn't care. I just wanted to get home. My head was spinning, and I was seeing things, but it was the alcohol, that's all. I'd been drinking. Way too much this time. That was all. I just had to get into bed, sleep it off.

When I woke up, everything would be better.

Then I was in my apartment. The bed was in a different place from what I remembered. Why didn't I remember rearranging my room? I must have done it recently. Damn alcohol. That's what it was. Was I getting that bad? I'd have to slow down before it was too late. I promised I would slow down.

Why did it feel as though I was bargaining?

The television was on again. Hadn't I turned it off? Did I have the timer set to keep turning it on? I turned it off. Again. I looked at the clock. 2:20. Was that right? Who cared?

I climbed into bed. Did I take my boots off, or did I never have them on? (Have I mentioned who cares?) I just needed to get some sleep.

Why was I so cold?
Sleep pulled white over my mind like a thin sheet.
I just wanted it to be right.
I'm close. So close.
Until that blasted talking wakes me up.

SUPPRESSION BY THE RIVER

The memories come back in a rush, and he grasps at the curious threads and tries to assemble them before he loses them again. Something is there, an incident it seems, long forgotten.

He was walking through these woods, along this creek. He remembers a mood. Is it the end of his high school years?

Yes, that must be it. He remembers feeling grown and strong, independent, but still young and awkward.

He remembers an autumn day, the waning sun shining through the red and orange leaves, dappling the ground.

Someone was with him. Someone, yes, but no, not one of his friends. Someone else.

His forehead creases in thought. A darker presence. A bully? An enemy? Yes. That seems right. But how? Why?

The flashes come faster. He remembers careful planning. In his mind he sees red on metal, the white of bone. He hears a grating thump.

A panic chills over him, and suddenly he scrambles to unravel the threads of memories, to bury them again in the soft earth by the river.

He remembers now: He forgot this on purpose.

THE BLACK AND CHURNING
SEA

A s the sea rose, the people of the town tried valiantly to stop it. They raised the breakers and extended the sea walls, but the waters kept rising. Day by day, more and more of the beach slipped under the waves.

At the town meetings, the older residents insisted on saving the town at any cost. "This has always been our home," they said. The younger people grumbled amongst themselves.

But the waters continued to rise. The waves bit into the edges of the town, engulfing the sea wall, and still the sea continued to rise. People saw their efforts were in vain, and the town was abandoned.

On the night the last old man left, he stopped by the cemetery to say goodbye to his wife, who had passed on so many years before. With the sound of the waves rushing toward him in the darkness, he paused a moment to trace his fingertips over the cool, rough surface of the headstone.

As he drove away, he could see in his rearview mirror the water tearing away the cemetery and sweeping black caskets out into the churning sea.

OH, GEE

He's getting gas, lost in his own thoughts, and he doesn't hear them roll up behind him.

"Look here, guys," he hears a rough voice say. "Looks like we got a gangster."

He flinches hard, but manages to regain his composure before turning to look at them, as nonchalantly and nonthreateningly as he can. There are four of them. Tank top. Baggy jeans. Cigarette. Pimp hat. They've parked at the pump behind him. Pimp hat works the pump, fills the car. Tank top and baggy jeans sit on the hood, one foot up on the bumper. Cigarette goes around the other side of his car, looking in through his windows.

"Hi, guys," he says, his voice anything but calm. "What's up?"

Cigarette shades his eyes to see into the driver's side window. Tank top nods at him, says, "That a prison tat?"

He looks at his arm. "Uh, yeah." He pulls his head back with a stupid grin. "You know."

"How you know what I know?"

He blinks. "Uh, I don't, I guess."

Cigarette calls to his friends, "Check it out. CD player."

Baggy jeans looks over to Cigarette, back to him. "Rich man, huh? Made it big?"

"Not that rich." He swallows. "Not that big."

Tank top steps off the bumper, walks up to him. "Well, rich man, what do you think? You gonna help out the younger generation?"

He takes out his cell phone, pulls the antenna out with his teeth, punches in a speed dial with his thumb, all the while watching in his rear-view mirror.

"It's me," he says. "You'll never guess what just happened."

He pauses, listens, smiles.

"No, I wish. Pussy like that. Damn! No, I was just getting some gas, and these four young punks tried to gangster-up on me."

He listens again, nodding wisely to himself.

"They thought so, but they didn't know who they was dealing with."

Nodding and smiling.

"That's right. O.G. An original."

He sits up in his seat, looks from the rear-view back over his shoulder quickly, shakes it off.

"Yeah, I should have. I let 'em know. They found out."

He looks forward again, steering now with his wrist on the wheel.

"I gave 'em twenty dollars so I wouldn't have to kick their asses."

Eyes are getting sleepy.

"Yeah. You know how it is."

GHOST RUNNER

They say that on his twelfth birthday he saw the Olympic marathon runners on television, and his mouth and eyes went wide. "It's just running!" he said. "I can do that."

And he did. He ran seven miles that afternoon, and every day from then on.

Two years later he became the captain of his high school cross-country team. The next summer he finished third in his first marathon. The next day he began training for the Olympics. "It's just running," he said. "I can do that."

That winter, a week before the regional race, shortly after dark, he was three miles into a run, on a long, sweeping curve. A minivan hit a patch of ice. The people of his town would wail at the world, but the dream died there in the snow.

Now, they say that on cold nights you can sometimes see a runner loping down the road. His footfalls make no sound, and his sweatshirt is smeared with blood. As you pass, he may turn to look at you, his neck at an odd angle. "It's just running," he'll say, his smile full of broken teeth. "I can do that."

SUNRISE

The night at the hotel dragged on like no other. Actually, this was kind of misleading. The fact was that, here in the heart of it, working behind the front desk in the bright lobby of this hotel, Larry Harrison could remember no other night. It felt as if this one night was the only life he had ever had. And it had been devoid of natural light.

Sometime in there, when it seemed the night was many years old, Larry wondered why he was here. He liked working in the hotel, sure, but did he have to work the audit? *Had* he even chosen it at all? Surrounded by darkness, he couldn't be sure. Maybe he had been born here in this lobby, with the lights inside and the television and the switchboard and the big glass windows holding back the shiny darkness. Late at night, it could seem that way sometimes.

Larry kept himself busy doing his job, keeping the coffee station loaded (though he was the only one drinking it), checking the intermittent chatter of the phone machine printer to catch errant long-distance calls (though the only activity was the usual local mischief, and even that was slow), and checking the rack against the computer printouts (though no one had come or gone since he had last checked it).

He was doing this last task when Douglas Dent, the security guard, came in through the front door. As he entered, a stiff breeze tried to pull the door from his grasp. The wind curled into the lobby like a viper, flittering the garland and rustling the ornaments on the tree beside the television.

Larry looked up from his position behind the desk. "Wow," he said. "That's a cold breeze."

Douglas grunted. "You're telling me," he said. He pulled the door closed behind himself and turned to Larry, stomping his feet. "Imagine if you had to walk around out in it."

Larry looked up at him with a wry smile. "No thanks."

Douglas went over to the couch corral and stood looking at the television. The sound was turned down, and the announcers mouthed the current headlines. Douglas watched for a moment, squeezing his hands together, then turned to the front desk.

Larry found himself turned away from the rack, leaning against the desk with the printed report slack in his hand. It wasn't good to stare at the darkness. He knew that. It couldn't be changed, and it wasn't good to throw wishes into it.

"Finished with the audit?" Douglas asked.

Larry pulled his thoughts back into the room with surprising reluctance. He looked at Douglas blankly, then down at the report in his hand. "Ah," he said. "It's been done, actually. I'm just re-running the rack to stay busy."

Douglas nodded understandingly. "Tired?"

Larry shook his head and sighed. "Not really. It's just ... the night is dragging on. It seems like it's been dark forever."

"I know what you mean," Douglas said, smiling now. "I thought it would never get done."

As Douglas put his radio, keys, and report on the desk, Larry felt an unexpected pang of jealousy. "Going home?"

Douglas was already back to the front door. "Yep," he said. "See you tomorrow."

The cold wind swirled into the lobby again, then Douglas was gone. Larry glanced at the clock with a frown. It was still only ten to four. Douglas was leaving ten minutes early. "Must be nice," Larry muttered.

Larry put away the keys and radio, put the report into the stack of other daily reports for the manager, and went back to checking the rack. Then he checked the coffee. And in there he watched the phone printout.

The night dragged on. Larry tried not to think about it. He just kept doing his job.

A while later, the automatic wake-up calls began, and the phone computer added them to its printout. A few men in suits —Larry guessed them to be salesmen—came down to check out. Someone turned up the volume on the news channel on the television.

Then, some time later, or maybe after no time at all, Larry found himself frowning again out the big window, out across the front parking lot to the mountains on the distant horizon. Silently, unannounced amid all the noise and bustle, and without any fuss, the sun had begun to rise.

The morning sunlight touched Larry's face, and he felt his frown begin to melt into a smile.

MEN AND WOMEN

HOT SUMMER NIGHT

I am told that, though it was a hot summer evening and Hubert had parked at the edge of the farm, the overpowering smell inside the car was that of his Bryll Cream.

With the car stopped, he set the radio, then turned sideways in the seat to put his arm around Rhonda, a big smile on his face. "I got some Jim Beam there in the glove box," he said. "You want some?"

Rhonda shook her head, brunette ringlets dancing. "Are you sure it's safe here?"

"Sure," he said. "I bring—I come out here by myself sometimes to listen to music."

She looked at him a long moment, then snuggled in against his arm, gazing at the sunset out across the fields.

"Someday, I aim to get me a farm just like this one," Hubert said in a soft, dreamy tone. "Barn. Silo. Front porch."

Rhonda looked at him, a faraway smile glittering in her eyes.

The sun finished setting, the radio played on, and the evening passed quietly into legend.

And later, in the sweltering darkness of the vinyl back seat, next to that Oklahoma farm, I was conceived.

ON THE BEACH

They strolled along the beach, the sand warm under their feet, the sun high and warm overhead in an azure sky, the white foam dancing off the blue waves rolling up to shore, the call of the seagulls cutting like shrill music through the puffy breeze. In his hand he felt the warmth, the comfort, the steadiness of hers.

Can I ask you a question? he asked. He was afraid that the sound of his voice would ruin the perfect serenity around them, but he'd been thinking about this for a long time, and he needed to ask.

He felt her smile at him in perfect acceptance. Of course he could ask her.

Are you ... glad you married me? He felt pressure in his face now, but he wouldn't let that become tears.

When he'd thought about the question earlier, he had not known the answer. He had remembered the quarrels, the petty fights over money, over time spent at work, over things he couldn't even remember anymore. He'd remembered all the ways things could have been different, and maybe better. And he had not known.

Here, serene on the beach, she told him something different. She reminded him of their days in college, staying alone together at the dorm over the Christmas break and dancing in stilettos in the snow. She brought back the green and white images of their wedding, and sneaking up to the hotel roof with a bottle of wine and a blanket on their honeymoon. He felt her hand squeeze his as she reminded him of their life together, the steady support they'd always found in each other, the comfort there.

Yes, he heard her say, she would always be happy she'd married him.

He looked down at the sand now. Do you wish that we'd had children? he asked.

He felt her smile reassuringly at him. We've talked about this before, he heard her say. Now is the time to accept our choices, find joy in the good things. Now is not the time for regrets.

Yeah, he said. Me, too.

If he thought about this, he would probably break down. There was never a little version of her running through the summer grass, asking for help with homework, or pinning on a graduation cap. And there never would be. With all his heart, he wished that was different.

Hey, he heard her say. Isn't this the beach we came to on our first real date?

He swallowed hard again against emotion. Yes, yes it is.

It's so warm and wonderful! It's just the way I remember it.

I was hoping, he said, brazenly foolish against the universe. I was hoping that by coming here, I could go back—that *we* could go back—and do it all over. I can't believe it all went by so quickly.

He couldn't hold the emotion back anymore. He tipped his chin to his chest as tears slid down his face and dropped onto the sand. He turned to face the ocean. Looking back where they'd walked, he saw a single set of footprints leading up to him on the beach. Already, he couldn't see back to where there were two sets of footprints.

I can't believe it's over.

It's okay, he heard her say, comforting. It's okay. It will never be over. Do what you came here to do.

He nodded at this, blinked back the tears, and walked out a little way into the water.

His feet in the crystalline sand, the waves lapping up his shins to his knees, he stood with all of paradise, it seemed, behind him. He held the ceramic jar under his left arm, cradled in his hand. His right hand now held the lid, cautiously, close to the open top of the urn.

One more question.

Yes?

How can I let you go?

Her voice called to him now, reached across the fabric of space and time, threading itself through the cry of the seagulls: *You never can.*

Blinking in the sun, tears streaming down his cheeks, he raised the urn high up in front of him, and the wind picked up at his back. His hands and arms felt numb as the urn tipped forward. The ashes came racing out, twisting into the wind and the ocean, spiraling high over his head and curling around his feet. He raised his head to sky and heaven and screamed with energy to shake the whole of the universe.

I never will!

SOMETIMES SHE COMES

S ometimes she comes to me in the night, slinking into the room as a cat, her hands trembling, her body eager, and our bodies twist together in a quiet crescendo of hushed excitement and an explosion of ecstasy like I have never experienced before.

Other times she does not come at all, and those nights I sleep little, my breathing shallow as I listen hard into the darkness, never giving up hope till the gray dawn presses against the back of the curtains of the tiny guest bedroom.

Every time the farmer welcomes me into his home, and when we retire after dinner to lemonade on the porch, he reminds me that he trusts me, but that he also owns a shotgun, and that hogs have a taste for human flesh.

The people at the office wonder why I return to this tiny burg, where the prospects seem so slim for a modest Bible salesman, and I never tell them of the generosity of the farmer, or his daughter.

Tonight my pulse quickens in eager anticipation as I hear the tiny creak of the doorknob.

Then I hear the unmistakable signature sound of a pump-action shotgun racking a shell into the chamber, and I wish I had told the people at the office where I was staying.

WAY DOWN IN THE VALLEY

Way down in the valley, the town locals were tearing up another Saturday night in the bars, the legion, the bowling alley. Up here on the peaceful hill, we were, literally and figuratively, above all that. We sat on wicker chairs on the back porch, sipping a fine Tempranillo and enjoying the quiet darkness of the back yard. A gentle breeze rustled the woods around us.

"I tell you," I told her, "this is so nice."

"Mm-hmm," she said.

"I mean, I worked hard for this—we both did. It's nice to finally have it, to be able to enjoy it. The fruits of our labor."

She swirled the dark liquid in her glass, inhaled it, took a drink.

I waved my glass out at the darkness, and by extension, at the riff-raff below. "Those people, they'll never have anything like this to appreciate."

She swatted at her leg. "I'm getting bit up by mosquitoes."

"Yeah," I said. I reached for the bottle and poured another generous portion into my glass. "Up here, we've got this fine wine, this beautiful landscaping." I waved in the direction of the landscaping, which was somewhere in the moist darkness beyond the ring of light from our back porch. "Down there, what have they got? Bowling and beer."

She was staring out at the darkness. "I like bowling," she said quietly.

"Yeah," I said. "Beer's good, too."

We sat quietly for a few minutes, drinking our expensive wine in large swallows.

"You want to go?" she asked.

I tipped the last of the wine down my throat. "I'll get the balls."

She was already out of her seat, wicker chair flying back against the wall. "I'll get my sweater."

CORNERSTONE

H oward traced his hand over the cool glass of the display case, peering intently inside at the cold steel and glittering gems. Light music wafted from the speakers inside the store, not the original songs, but instrumental impostors. This bothered him.

His attention, though, was focused inside the display case, and his stomach was in knots. Fucking diamonds, he thought. One of the most abundant of gems, ridiculously marketed up to three months' salary.

Still, it was tradition and all.

"Can I help you?" asked the voice behind the counter.

Howard glanced up at the owner of the voice. Fuck, he thought, the prices they charge, they could at least have decent uniforms. The clerk behind the counter wore dark slacks and a maroon polo shirt, with a crooked name tag. Crooked, like it was hastily put in place of a forgotten one. Evidently a *borrowed* name tag that said "Steve." Was nothing real here?

"Yeah, Steve," said Howard, "you can help me." He pointed to the rings in the case, tapped his fingernail on the glass. "How good are these?"

"Oh, they're very nice, sir. Very good indeed.".

Howard stared at the rings for a long moment. "She won't be able to tell?"

"Does she own a jeweler's loupe?"

"No."

Steve—or whatever—put on a genuinely smug face. "Then she won't be able to tell, sir."

Howard nodded, hating himself. "I'll take it," he said.

"Excellent, sir." Steve reached into the case.

"No, not that one." Harold's stomach felt cold. "The one at the bottom."

A pause. "The small one?"

Harold tried very hard not to wince. "Yes."

STAIRS APART

Upstairs, he could hear her turn off the shower. That was going to be a hard one for her to explain. Why would she say she had needed to take a shower at nine o'clock in the evening? What reason would she give? What was her *real* reason?

And why couldn't he stop her? Why couldn't he keep her here, at home? She was his wife, after all. He should be able to keep her from going out to—wherever it was she was going. Why couldn't he stop her?

Why wouldn't she stop, for him?

Every night it was the same. Every night it was a different excuse.

Downstairs, in the darkness of their rented townhome, his clothes felt as though they were hanging off him like burlap sacks. He felt like a shrunken old man, a worn-out man in the clothes of a virile younger man, the man he used to be, in clothes that used to fit him.

He could feel himself sweating. His senses heightened, he felt every beat of his heart in the tight mass of tension that was his chest.

She would be leaving tonight, of course. Of course. But where was she going? And what was she doing there?

A lover, perhaps? He thought maybe. Wherever she was going, it was inconceivable that she would be alone. Was she showering, now, for a lover?

Upstairs he heard her switch off the light. She would come downstairs now, and she would have a reason to leave, a reason to go somewhere. She was leaving him, and he was powerless to stop her.

In a moment she would be downstairs, never looking at him, leaving. He would ask her where she was going, and why she had to go, and she would lie to him. She would say she was going to the grocery store for some important last-minute food. Or she would say that she was going to meet a girlfriend who had an all-important crisis. Or she would say that she had to visit her brother, who needed her help urgently. Or she would say that she was going to the park to think.

Never looking at him.

Lies. All of it, lies.

She would return, of course, as she did every night. Later. No matter how vigorously he waited watching the door, or how indifferently he studied the late-night television, she would return later, with an excuse and a story that wouldn't pan out if he checked them.

Never looking at him.

Every night it was the same. Every night it was the same. Every night it was the same. Every night it was different. But every night it was the same.

Upstairs, he heard her footsteps coming down the short hall to the steps. Her footsteps, approaching yet leaving him.

Downstairs, in the darkness, his heart was breaking.

WHY THEY HAVE THAT RULE
ANYWAY

Gregory Stanton pulled the door closed and waited. At first it was pitch black, and he felt swamped by the rolling colors and hums inside his own head. He stood without moving, not knowing where anything was. He wished he'd sat down or memorized the room before closing the door, but then this whole thing was misplanned and crazy.

He was going to do it anyway, and so he stood in the dark and waited for his eyes to adjust, listening to the footsteps outside.

The guy at the front desk started out calm. "I need to know what room Lynn Stanton is in," he said, calmly.

Larry's shift had started at eleven the previous evening. It was now nearly six in the morning, and even though he had a fresh cup of coffee on the desk in front of him, he was tired. All the same, his professionalism stayed in top form. He was proud of that.

Larry looked down at the room list on his desk and located

the name "Stanton, Lynn". The list said the room was registered to two adults. He reached over to the rack and pulled out the registration card, careful to shield all his actions to not give away the room number. As he had expected, the room was registered to two people, but only one name was given: hers. Husband or not, unless his name was listed on the registration card, he wasn't the information.

"I'm sorry, sir," Larry said. "I can't give you the room number. If you'd call... perhaps from the house phone... I could put you through to the room, but I can't give you the room number."

The man, who looked as tired as Larry felt, ran a hand through his thick brown hair, where parallel grooves made it look like he'd been doing that all night. "She's my wife," he said. "I know that she's here, her car's parked out back."

Larry thought he understood what was going on: the man and his wife had intended to meet here, and now she had registered the room, and he wanted to go up to meet her. It was very nice, and very ordinary, but it ran straight up against the rules of the hotel. "I'm sorry, sir," Larry repeated. "I can't give you the room number, but I could call the room and ask—"

"No!" the man said with sudden energy. "No, I don't want you to call the room, I just want to know what room she's in."

Something started to turn cold in Larry's stomach. "I'm sorry, sir, but I can't give you the room number."

"But I'm her husband..." the man said.

The man, now gripping the edge of the front desk very hard, turned squarely to face Larry, giving him the distinct impression that he was trying to intimidate him. Some people found Larry's bald head threatening. This man did not seem to be one of those people. Larry nonchalantly stepped back away from the desk, to lean against the back counters. The man seemed to be on the verge of exploding. If he did, Larry wanted to be out of reach of the shrapnel.

Larry thought something very different now about what was going on here, and this was exactly why room numbers were not to be given out. "I'm sorry, sir—"

"I'm her husband! You have to tell me what room she's in."

Larry didn't say anything. He was now fairly sure that nothing he could say was going to please this man. Plus, he didn't like being interrupted.

The man at the front desk was clearly fuming now, his face red. He seemed to be trying to think of some argument that would persuade Larry to give him the number. Or maybe he was thinking of coming over the desk and getting it for himself.

Larry tried not to think about it. However, if it came to that, Larry was twenty-seven, tall-ish, and lean. The man at the desk looked to be in his late thirties, short-ish, and a bit paunchy. Probably that gave Larry the edge. All the same, Larry wished someone else would come into the lobby.

"I'll call the cops," the man said suddenly.

Larry thought this was a splendidly stupid idea. "Okay," he said.

The man turned on his heel and went through the door to the pay-phone in the little room that served as the night lobby. Larry saw him pick up the phone and dial three numbers: 911. Larry almost smiled to himself. He was going to get no assistance from that person, either.

Just then, a guest came into the lobby with an ordinary request: to check out. While Larry took the key, checked the charges, and bade the guest farewell, he could hear the person he was now referring to in his interior monologue as "the crazy man" talking to someone on the phone. From the rising tone of his voice, he was getting exactly the level of assistance that Larry had thought he would get.

By the time Larry had checked the guest out of the computer system, turned off the phone in the room, and marked the room as a checkout on the executive housekeeper's tally sheet, the crazy man was gone, disappeared out of the night lobby and out of sight somewhere in the parking lot.

Larry wondered for a few minutes if he should do something about the crazy man, and if so, what. Douglas Dent, the security guard at the Empire Hotel, had gone home when his shift ended at five. The manager, though he lived on the property, would not be awake yet. In the end, he decided he should simply pass a warning on to Gertrude when she came in to take over behind the front desk. Without the assistance of a front desk person, the crazy man had no way of finding out the room number of his wife, unless he went door-to-door knocking. And if he did that, everyone would know soon enough.

❦

Gertrude was going over the day's reservations when Sam Twain, the manager of The Empire Hotel, walked in and looked around. "He's here late," Sam said.

Gertrude looked up at Sam to see him staring through the big front windows, evidently at Larry, who had just walked out the front door to go home. She glanced up at the clock behind her on the wall. 7:25. "Yeah," she said.

"Anything wrong?"

Gertrude stood up, put a hand on one hip, and looked through the front windows herself. Larry was just getting into his car. "Just Larry being Larry."

Sam chuckled at this. "Larry suspicious of something again?"

"Ain't he always?"

Sam nodded and turned back toward the door leading to his

office. "You have to admire someone who takes his job so seriously."

"I guess," said Gertrude.

Sam stopped at the doorway and glanced once again around the empty lobby. Suddenly he frowned. "Is that new trainee here yet?"

"Not yet," Gertrude said, "I told him to come on in at eight, but if I know my nephew, he'll be here ten minutes early."

Sam nodded, evidently satisfied that all was well with the world. "Well, I have to go out this morning—we're almost all out of coffee—but tell him I'll give him a tour of the place when I get back."

"Sure thing, boss."

❧

Brian Hauser looked back toward the door that led to the office area. His aunt Gertrude was not back from the bathroom yet. Mr. Twain wasn't back from the store yet. The housekeepers had arrived at the same time he did, but they, of course, were not at the front desk, and, being housekeepers, would not have been helpful anyway. He was going to have to handle this on his own.

He turned back to the short-ish, slightly paunchy man at the front desk. "Stanton, you said, right?"

The man ran his fingers through his hair and licked his lips. "That's right," he said. "Lynn Stanton."

Brian traced his finger down the guest roster. "Ah, yes. I have her right here." He looked up uncertainly at the man in front of him. "You say you're her husband?"

"Yes. She was getting the room. I'm supposed to be meeting her here."

Brian straightened himself up and put on his official voice. "I'll need to see some ID."

"Of course." The man pulled out his wallet and slid his driver's license across the cool marble of the front desk.

Brian picked it up, read the name very carefully, and slid the license back to the man. "Very well, Mr. Stanton. The room is 314. I'll go and get you a key, but I will need an additional five dollars for the key deposit for the extra key."

Mr. Stanton was smiling very large. "That's perfectly okay."

৩৯৫

Gregory Stanton looked both ways down the hall, seeing no one. He listened intently at the door of room 314, but could hear nothing but the pounding of his own heart. He gripped the doorknob with his right hand, the brushed steel smooth and cool under his fingertips. With his left hand he eased the key into the lock, one careful tick at a time.

Tick.

All her lies, all the lies she thought worked just because they couldn't be disproven. Well, she was about to get proof. How was she going to continue to deny she had a boyfriend when she was caught in bed with him?

Tick.

Her so-called boss at the supermarket, that was who it had to be. Whenever they were working together, she "forgot" that she was working late. And every time Gregory got sent out of town, the neighbors told him her car never came home. Well, he'd come back early this time, and he'd found where her car was parked.

Tick.

The key seated fully in the lock. Gregory Stanton could feel his breath almost wet in his throat. He tested the key. It turned.

Gently, slowly, he eased the knob all the way over. Then, with one final glance both ways down the hall, he took his little handgun out of his back pocket and burst into the room.

It was empty.

He almost screamed even though it was empty, then he almost screamed *because* it was empty.

Empty!

He pushed the door closed behind him, then leaped around the room like a movie cop, thrusting the gun into every new area—the space behind the door, the far side of the bed, the bathroom, behind the bathroom door, the tub.

Empty.

His brain wound down a notch, and he started looking around the room for evidence of what might be happening.

The one queen-sized bed had been used, that was obvious, but whether by one person, or two, or a whole troop, he couldn't tell. His eyes wandered to the dresser top. A white plastic ice bucket held some water and some sad scraps of ice cubes. Beside the dresser was a garbage can. In the garbage can were some soda cans. Was this the evidence he was looking for? He didn't know.

He had the idea suddenly to check how many bath towels had been used, and went over to check it out.

Just as he got to the bathroom door, he heard a key in the lock. Before he could even think, he had launched himself through the bathroom door and closed himself into the pitch-blackness of the bathroom.

His left hand reached out to find the surface of the door, to keep his balance. His right hand still held his gun, and the trigger felt hard under his finger.

Alice Johnson made her rounds quickly and efficiently, clipboard in hand. As the executive housekeeper, it was her job to verify all the checked-out rooms before the housekeepers got to them. She would make sure the rooms were empty, turn off the televisions, open the curtains, and make sure there were no surprises waiting for her girls.

Today, at eight-thirty in the morning, not many guests had checked out of the third floor yet. She found no surprises, and she had time to pull off the sheets and pile up the towels, little touches that would save her girls time later.

The last new room to check was 314. As she opened the door, she had a strange sensation of movement, but saw nothing. She paused for a second at this, then proceeded cautiously. "Hello?" she said.

No response.

It must have been her imagination.

The television was already off. She crossed the room and pulled the curtains open wide. New brightness flooded the room. She pulled the comforter and blankets off the bed, dropping them at the foot of it. With a couple of practiced tugs, she whipped the sheets off the bed without disturbing the mattress pad. She dropped them into a pile just outside the door, then headed to the bathroom to get the towels.

Later, she would remember seeing a flash of light and a puff of smoke.

❦

"So he just fired as soon as she opened the door?" Douglas Dent asked. "He just came out of the bathroom, guns blazing?"

Larry was comparing a room status printout to the cards on the rack, torn between wanting to talk about the crazy incident with someone, and wishing Douglas would go somewhere and iron his uniform. "He didn't really come out at all, from what I heard. He just panicked and squeezed the trigger too hard when she opened the door." He made the motion with his hand. "Bullet went right into the floor."

Douglas seemed to think this was funny. "Down into the room below?"

"No, it was just a little gun, and the bullet barely made it through the carpet."

"Bet it scared Alice pretty good, though, huh?"

"Probably."

Douglas shook his head at the insanity of it all, then got up and walked over to the front desk.

"So how did the guy get in the room in the first place?" Douglas asked, leaning on the front desk to watch Larry. "Did they leave the room open or what?"

Larry explained how the whole series of events had come together, including how he had bravely stood up to the crazy man when he had threatened to come over the desk and take the key.

Douglas was smiling. "Did Sam fire the new guy?"

Larry shook his head in disgust. "Gertrude made a big deal about how I should have left a note on the registration card and got Sam to let him off about it."

"So where was the guy's wife, anyway? Did she see him coming and take off?"

"That's the really dumb part. Lynn Stanton's room was 341, but Brian read the number wrong and gave him the key to 314 instead."

"What an idiot."

"Yeah, and after the police came and arrested Gregory Stanton, his wife came down and paid for another night."

Douglas's mouth fell open. "They're still here? In 341?"

"Yep. She won't bail him out, so he's still in jail, and she's still here."

Douglas straightened up, paced to the front doors and back. "Not your typical Wednesday morning," he said, sagely.

Larry shrugged. "I've had worse."

TURNING POINT

On their last evening in Paris, they walked along the boulevard with brisk autumn gusts swirling leaves about their feet. "I'm telling you," he said, taking her gloved hand into his, "this vacation has been ... inspirational."

She smiled at him with a warmth he had not seen in a long time and did not pull her hand away. "Yes, it has," she said.

"When we get back, everything's going to be different." His free hand gestured in bold strokes. "New job, diet, exercise. Everything."

Weariness touched the corners of her hazel eyes.

"I know you've heard all this before," he said, gesturing more softly now, "but how could things be the same after ... the Eiffel Tower?"

Her eyes met his, connecting. "They can't."

The directness took him aback. "That's right," he said, nearly stumbling over the words. "Everything *will* be different. You'll see."

"I hope it is different," she said. She withdrew her hand from his. "And I hope I see it someday."

An arctic breeze blew between them.

"I'm not going back with you."

WORLD OF WHITE

I'm starting to think maybe the whole thing was a bad idea. It's not my fault, though. I've done everything that I could. It's her. From the start, she has done everything she could to embarrass me, to make me look bad. All I ever wanted to give her was my heart. I couldn't give it to her literally, so instead, I gave her something else, something, it seems now, almost as valuable.

It started two months ago, a month after I got here. I was coming out of the dorm, on my way to communication class, when I saw her. I stopped in my tracks. People bumped into me, but I didn't care. She was the most amazing thing I'd ever seen. Her black hair billowing in the breeze, those green eyes—wow.

So I followed her. I ditched my communication class and I followed her. It turned out she was going to a psychology class, and I waited outside her classroom door. When she came out, I said to her, "You are the most amazing person I have ever known, and it is our destiny to be together."

She laughed at me, then frowned when she saw I was serious, then walked away quickly, glancing back fearfully at me every few steps. None of that amused me.

Immediately it became my mission to make her see what I already knew, that we were meant to be together. I followed her. I snooped through her trash. I sneaked into the dorm room next to hers and listened to her through the wall. I was so clever.

One night, I even slipped out the window of the common room of her dorm suite and crept along the ledge until I was outside her window. It was there, three floors above the grassy back lot behind Main Gate B, that my heart was broken. She was not alone. There was a guy with her, and they were occupied. The lights were off in her room, but in the ambient light of the moon and the courtyard lights, I could see glimpses of flesh through the window. What I saw both aroused and sickened me. She was naked, and that was delightful, but she was with another man, a man older than me, probably twenty-two. Suave and sophisticated.

I wanted to throw up. I wanted to smash through the window. I thought, very seriously, about jumping.

But there, with one foot on the ledge, one foot already stepped out into space and my fingertips slipping on the rough surface of the bricks, I had an epiphany. I realized what I had to do. If she was involved with someone else, I had only to convince her that I was meant for her, that I wanted her more than her current boyfriend. And as my gaze fell upon the neon sign of the tattoo parlor in the distance down the street, I thought of something so perfect, so convincing, so crazy that it just might work.

I had found out (how could she stop destiny?) that her name was Rachel.

"What will it be?" the tattoo guy asked.

I told him.

"Are you kidding?"

I told him I was not.

"I can't do that!"

I offered him double.

He did it.

It hurt like hell.

The next morning I was waiting for her when she came out of the dorm, on her way to the psychology class again. "I want to show you something," I said.

My approach startled her. Her eyes searched the path for a way to avoid me and found me blocking the sidewalk. She looked up at me, exasperated and expectant.

I reached my hands up to my face, gripped my eyelids between my thumbs and forefingers, and flipped them back up on themselves, exposing their pink insides. The maneuver was quite painful, but it revealed my absolute commitment and devotion to her. Tattooed across the right was "I LOVE", and across the left, "RACHEL".

She saw it. She read it. She cringed.

"I did it for you," I said.

She was speechless.

"Don't you see?" I said. "It proves that we're meant to be together. Who else could ever have this level of devotion?"

She stepped back away from me on the sidewalk. "Leave me alone," she said. She drew her books across her chest defensively.

"Wait," I said, but just then another girl came up behind her on the sidewalk. As she tried to get past me, her eyes came up to mine.

"Wow," she said. "That's totally freaky."

"What do you know about anything?" I asked. I tried to turn away to Rachel, but she was already gone. She fled back into the dorm, leaving me on the sidewalk, alone and embarrassed and frustrated, but not daunted.

Slowly, over the next few days and weeks, that changed. Rachel refused to see me. She stopped going to classes for a while, and I think she even left campus for a week or so. I wrote her long letters explaining why I did it, and how it proved everything she ever needed to know about me, about us. I slipped the letters under the door of her dorm room late at night, but she never acknowledged them. I tried to tell her in person, of course, but I was never able to get close to her.

Gradually, I began to fear that perhaps I had made a mistake. For one thing, I could see the tattoos when I closed my eyes in bright light. I couldn't quite read them, but I knew they were upside down to me when my eyelids were normal. I was the only person who appreciated the work, and it was upside down so me. Plus, the ink had penetrated through my eyelids to the other side, the side visible with my eyelids flipped down normally. But instead of a testimony of love, it was simply blotchy points of ink.

But then, when I was at the end of my rope, I had another epiphany. I awoke one morning with the brilliant idea of how I could make sure Rachel got the message, how I could demonstrate beyond any doubt my love for her. It would be more painful than anything else I would likely ever experience, but it would be worth it to prove my love, and to win hers.

That evening I gave myself a generous dose of liquid painkiller—whiskey—and set to work. I went into the bathroom with my Swiss Army knife and got out the scissor tool. Three minutes later, I had clipped them off and used super glue to suture the wounds. It was a mess. Who would have known eyelids to have so much blood? But it was a success.

By morning I had tanned the eyelids in a bath of vinegar, then carefully mounted them on a wooden base using toothpicks to hold them up like banners so the message could be read as the expression of eternal devotion that it was: I LOVE RACHEL.

I left it on the floor outside her dorm room for her to find first thing when she came out of her room.

It didn't work as well as I had hoped. In fact, she seems to have taken it the wrong way altogether. I never thought I'd have to explain the message to her, but that's what I've been doing for the past several days. Trying to, anyway. The restraining order she got has made certain things inconvenient, but I won't let a legal technicality stand in the way of true love.

Since that morning, I've been living in a world of white. I can't close my eyes completely, and the incessant light has strained my retinas, or something like that. Everything now seems like I'm seeing it through a milky fog. The price of love, they say, is steep, but this side effect is not one I saw coming. I tried to fashion myself some artificial eyelids using pieces of leather from the tongue of one of my boots, but so far I've had only limited success with it.

Removing my eyelids may have been a mistake, but I know what to do next. The mistake with the first tattoo was that the message was too short, too simple. No wonder she didn't believe it, it didn't spell out any kind of rational argument. My next solution will explain everything in detail.

Yes, it's another tattoo, but this time it's better. This time, I'll be getting the tattoo on a flabby section of my thigh. I've checked it out, and I'm pretty sure that I'll be able to get the skin to grow back after I cut it out if I just keep the area covered with plastic wrap. It will be painful, sure, but isn't true love worth it? I think it is. I think it's worth any price, and I'm willing to pay for the reward. And when she sees the testimony written out on parchment of my own making, how can she deny it? It's the perfect plan.

I've already bought the whiskey.

LIFE AND DEATH

THE DEATH OF KARMA

She was the kind of person who, when looking through her closet for used clothes to donate to the women's shelter, inevitably came out with an armful of new blouses, unable to consider giving someone else less than what she kept for herself. She was the kind of woman who would give her change to a coworker if he looked hungry and the vending machine wasn't taking dollar bills. One time I saw her give her lunch to a man with a "homeless veteran" sign at the exit ramp on her way to work, because the genuine hunger she saw in his gaunt features plucked at the strings of her heart. This is what I am thinking of when the casket is lowered into the ground and her children drop handfuls of dirt into the hole. They say the good things you do will come back to you in the end. This is what I am thinking of as we turn to go, and the sky is gray and flat as the bottom of an iron, and great drops of cold rain begin to fall in dark splotches on the bright autumn leaves.

ABOVE THE FIELD OF
BUTTERCUPS

The brown Town Car glided to a stop at the side of the gravel road next to a wide field of golden buttercups, its passenger side wheels crunching into the shallow ditch beside the road. Nothing could be seen through the dark amber tint of its windows. A thin haze of dust rolled over the car for a moment as the driver put the car in park and turned off the engine. The car's taillights glowed briefly through the dust cloud, then were dark.

The driver's door opened, and a barrel-chested man wearing an ill-fitting blue suit stepped out. Smoothing down the strained buttons on the front of his jacket with one hand, he looked up and down the road, deliberately casual. Satisfied, he nodded his head to the open door of the car.

At this, the passenger side door on the back swung open, and a lean man with gray eyes and a cold expression stepped from the car. His dark blue suit seemed exquisitely tailored. He, too, took a casual look around, then gestured at the open back door.

A third man climbed from the Town Car. A purple bruise grew on the cheekbone under his left eye. His brown suit was wrinkled, his right sleeve torn a bit and missing the cuff link. This man had a narrow face with pointed features. He, too, looked up and down the country road, but with a bit of hope in his eyes. However, as his gaze found only the quiet sweep of field, the only movement their own wake of dust twisting and settling into the weeds beside the road, that hope faded, replaced with abject acceptance.

Beside the road lay a wide meadow of golden buttercups waving gently in the late-summer breeze. The field rose in a gentle slope, and on the other side, where the meadow gave way to deep silver birch woods, the slope rose to become a hill.

The gray-eyed man gestured toward the meadow and, late-afternoon sun at their backs, the three men set off across the field of buttercups, heading to the woods on the other side. They walked in silence, the only noise coming from the brush of flowers against their legs.

Halfway across the field, the three men stopped suddenly, their attention focused straight ahead. A glimmer of silver rose silently from behind the trees. As it rose, it became the rounded leading edge of a metal ring, turning slowly on thin spokes around a black hub. This was one of the G4 space stations, one of those in the lower orbits that were more expensive, but that let its occupants feel more connected to Earth. Larger and larger it grew, until it appeared twice as wide as the full moon. They could see, or thought they could, the gray rectangles of steel buildings along the inside edge of the disc. Even at this distance, tiny checkerboard patterns of crops were visible, tiny squares of tan and green.

"Hey, Sammy," said the weasel-faced man in the middle quietly. "Do you think there's a heaven?"

The gray-eyed lean man refused to make eye contact. "Shut up, Frankie," he said.

"I'm just saying," Frankie continued, his eyes fixed on the

disc of the space station overhead. "There's still stuff we don't know, right?" He looked briefly at the third man, who had been driving the car, for support. "You know what I mean, right, Joey?"

Sammy looked down at the ground. Joey stared up at the space station, his mouth hanging open.

"I mean," continued Frankie, "we've got these giant space stations up in the sky, and cities under the ocean. We've got outposts on other planets, other moons."

"Our moon, too," said Joey.

"Our telescopes have looked all the way back to the beginning of the universe. But—" His voice faltered. "There's still stuff we don't know, right?"

Sammy looked at the ground.

Joey said, "Uh."

"There still could be a heaven, right?"

No one said anything. Insects buzzed near the edge of the woods. The space station continued to wheel higher into the sky, glass and steel sparkling.

"Come on," said Sammy, stepping out again toward the woods, "we gotta go."

Frankie followed, with some hesitation, and Joey brought up the rear.

"You think so, though, don't you, Sammy?" Frankie asked. A measure of pleading had crept into his voice.

"Shut up, Frankie."

The space station climbed steadily into the sky. As the men walked, Frankie and Joey could not keep their eyes off the station. Sammy's eyes stayed on the silver birch trees at the edge of the field of buttercups.

The three men reached the edge of the meadow, entered the woods, and began to climb the hill. Overhead, the space station disappeared behind the shimmering canopy of leaves. Frankie and Joey strained to see the space station, catching glimpses of its silvery form in the snatches of blue sky between the glittering green leaves.

They had nearly reached the top of the hill, and the station had risen to almost directly above them, when Sammy stopped walking. "This is it," he said. "Here."

Frankie was breathing hard. He looked desperate and sad.

Joey took his eyes from the sky and closed his mouth.

"Hey, Sammy, Big T knows I'm sorry, right?"

"He knows, Frankie."

Frankie looked around at the woods as if looking for something.

Joey stood with his hands crossed in front of himself, facing Frankie squarely, his chest puffed out a bit.

Frankie said, "There's nothing else we can work out. Maybe just the three of us?"

Sammy reached inside his jacket. "I don't think so, Frankie."

A moment later, at the noise, a tiny flock of birds lit out from the tops of the birch trees like pepper thrown into the sky. Then all was quiet.

Sammy and Joey made their way back down the hill in silence. The leaves hissed and growled under their feet. The sun had almost completed its run to the horizon, and a chill had crept into the air of the forest. It would be dark soon.

They reached the edge of the woods and emerged into the soft yellow sunlight and the field of buttercups. The space station was visible again, spinning now down toward the far horizon on a course that would intersect the sun.

Joey's eyes found the space station and stayed on it as they crossed the field. Right as they reached the road and the car again, the space station crossed in front of the sun in a kind of eclipse. For a long moment, the sunlight flickered and flared through the spokes of the ring, spraying spectrums through the glass of the buildings, dazzling beams off the steel. Joey blinked against the sun, pointing, his mouth open again.

Sammy glanced in the direction Joey was pointing. "Let's get out of here," he said. He reached for the door handle.

Joey stood still, watching the spectacle. The eclipse passed quickly, and the light on the other side was colder somehow. The station slid free of the sun, a flat ring falling to the horizon. Joey closed his mouth and turned to Sammy. "What do you think about that?" he asked.

"What?"

"That what Frankie was saying. About heaven. Do you think, maybe—"

"Shut up, Joey," Sammy said.

Sammy lit a cigarette while Joey went around to the driver's side. At the door, Joey paused and looked back at the field of yellow buttercups. The flowers had already swallowed up the path of their footsteps. On up the hill, the silver birch woods showed no sign of their presence. Sunlight glittered green and yellow as a breeze lifted the leaves.

"Frankie knows," Joey said suddenly, quietly.

Sammy looked at Joey with cold eyes, spat into the dirt, and got into the car.

Joey took one last look at the western horizon. The space station was a black ring now, plunging behind the hills below the sun. He watched until it had slipped from view, then got into the car. The sun would be gone soon. It would be very dark out here in the country.

MOMENT OF CLARITY

U p on the roof, he stepped carefully onto the ledge and sat down next to the stone gargoyle on the corner of the building, blinking in the light of the rising sun. Anyone who saw him might suppose he was considering throwing himself to his death, but the notion was ridiculous. He had never felt more alive.

He was forty-two, and today, for the first time, he felt he really understood his life: the politics of the office, his marriage, his own desires, all of it. In the crisp morning air, he recognized that the source of this new perspective and clarity was the death of his mother, coming as it had so soon after the death of his son. Sure, the path had been rocky, and the journey had ripped him apart, but it had reassembled him too, left him something bigger than he was before, something stronger. He felt, for the first time in a long time, invincible.

At that moment, with a rocky grinding noise, the gargoyle turned its head toward him. A stone hand reached out and give him a push.

They would say he jumped.

FRESH BACON

The Camaro finally pulled over next to a hillside dotted with fireflies. Officer Dodd approached the car with his senses alert and his hand on his gun. The driver seemed to be alone, but you always had to be careful, especially out here in the lonely foothills.

The tinted window whirred down. "Evening, Officer," came a smooth voice from inside. The driver had a mane of hair and a full beard, and his eyes and teeth glinted in the darkness.

"Evening," Dodd said. "Are you aware you were weaving across the lines back there?"

"Yes, sir."

"I had my lights on for more than a mile before you pulled over."

The driver smiled. "Yes, sir."

Dodd couldn't smell alcohol, but the driver's behavior was odd, to say the least. "Where are you going at this time of night?"

"Me and the boys are hungry ..."

"Wh—" Movement on the hillside caught Dodd's attention. The fireflies were moving, pairing up. Then they weren't fireflies, but eyes. Dozens of them.

And it was too late to draw his revolver. Too late, even, to scream.

A DARK AND STORMY NIGHT

I t was a dark and stormy night. In the doorway of the cabin on the little hill in the big woods, I smoked a cigarette and watched the tempest. Lightning flickered and danced over the trees. Rain fell in great black sheets, and the wind howled around the cabin. I'd come here to find peaceful solitude, and this was not it.

"Strange weather, isn't it, son?"

My heart skipped a beat at the sound of the voice. I turned to find my father standing behind me, looking over my shoulder out the door at the swirling storm. The yellow light of the gas lantern on the table by the door fell across his face, casting his wrinkled features into sharp relief. "Strange, indeed," I said.

"Would you say the wind or the rain is the strangest?" he asked.

I looked out at the blustering storm, then back into his wizened face. "Neither," I said. "The strangest part of the storm is you, here."

Lightning flashed in his eyes, and the shadows on his face twisted into a smile.

"After all," I continued, "you've been dead ten years."

STANDING ON THE THRESHOLD

I looked away from my father out the door at the storm. Lightning flashed overhead and crackled away over the treetops. The wind gusted a cool spray against my face. When I turned back to the cabin, the yellow light of the gas lantern flickered, and my father's eyes shone from deep shadows. "You shouldn't be here," I said quietly. "You're dead."

He nodded with a wry smile. "Nights like these, though," he said, glancing deliberately at the storm, "have a way of bringing us out."

I thought about this. "I almost didn't come up here at all, you know. The rain washed the road out in several places."

He nodded. "They'll find your jeep down there in the river." His voice was calm, like the soft grass over a grave. "Of course, after all this rain, they won't find it until spring."

I scoffed, out of breath. "You think I'll crash my Jeep on the way down the hill?"

I felt a chill through my bones, heard the gentle rush of distant water.

"No, son," he said, and his smile turned wistful. "You crashed on the way up."

BILLY VAIL

O ut over the eastern mountaintops, the sun splashed watercolor pink up into the pre-dawn blue of the sky, as it did every day, as it had every day for generations. In the brisk morning air, Billy Vail waited for his ride, kicking his feet to keep warm. With a low metallic groan, his city bus finally appeared. Its brakes screamed it to a stop in front of Billy Vail. As the first light of the new day touched the crown of his head, he stepped aboard.

His journey had started at the beginning of the bus route, right in the middle of town at Central Avenue. Now he was riding west, where the Avenues increased to the end of the journey.

At first, he was so tired he could barely stay awake. The pitching and rumbling of the bus kept him off balance. It wasn't until the bus rolled past First Avenue that he felt comfortable moving around on it.

The bus seemed to creep furiously slowly past the first eighteen or twenty avenues, the sun dragging slowly up into the sky. There was so much Billy Vail wanted to see along the bus route. He was practically bubbling over with excitement.

From time to time a girl would sit by Billy Vail for a while. Although they never stayed for long, Billy Vail was fond of each of them. He would always remember their names.

The sun approached its zenith and Billy Vail felt fresh and powerful. At Twenty-Third Avenue, a girl climbed up on the bus and quickly sat down next to Billy Vail. She smiled at him, and for a moment Billy Vail thought he could see forever in her eyes, and he couldn't catch his breath. Before the bus got to the next avenue, though, she got off. She tried to get Billy Vail to get off with her, to take another bus. He found himself wanting to. He thought about it as long as he could—the bus was not slowing down for him to think. In the end, he stayed on. It just seemed that the part of the city he wanted to see lay along the route of the bus he was on. Later, though, throughout his journey, he thought about that one radiant girl. Sometimes he wished there was a way he could go back and follow her. Many times, many times, he thought that that was the path he was supposed to have taken, and that he had missed his chance.

At Twenty-Seventh Avenue a mysterious blonde beauty climbed delicately aboard. She sat by Billy Vail. He felt comfortable with her next to him, and he thought she would ride with him for the rest of the trip. Strangely, though, he could never quite see how that would work out. Sadly, inexplicably, she seemed to feel the same thing.

Perhaps it wasn't a complete surprise, then, when she got off the bus at the next stop, Thirtieth Avenue. It hurt just the same.

Billy Vail watched her out the window for a long time. The bus rumbled on. Her features grew more indistinct as the distance increased. He could no longer see the traces of her face. Her scent evaporated in the air. For a while, it seemed that his heart was stretching out to her like a bungee cord, but then that feeling was gone, replaced by only absence. For a long time, he wished he could have gotten off with her.

When he finally turned back to the front, somewhere around Thirty-Third Avenue, he thought he felt the evening already approaching, although it was only mid-day.

One by one the landmarks Billy Vail had planned to see flashed by the side of the bus. Somewhere he noticed that the landmarks themselves were not quite as exciting as he had imagined they would be. Perhaps he was taking the wrong bus, and what he wanted to see lay along another route.

Consumed with worry and doubt over his trip, he didn't even notice when she got on the bus. He didn't notice when she took a seat near him. And he was completely surprised to find her in the seat next to him as the bus rumbled past Thirty-Fifth Avenue. She was a common-sense beauty with sharp raven eyes. Billy Vail smiled. Billy Vail thought it was about time. He felt like he had been riding forever.

The next many avenues passed through a school zone of sorts. The seats near Billy Vail were suddenly abuzz with children. Their laughter warmed Billy Vail's heart. The avenues were flashing by much more quickly now. There was nothing for Billy Vail to do but to squeeze the sharp-eyed girl's hand and hang on for the ride.

Before he realized it, the sun was pushing ahead of him in the sky. The sign for Fortieth Avenue caught him completely by surprise, and it seemed only a second later that he looked up and caught a glimpse of the sign for Forty-Fifth Avenue flashing past.

Billy Vail almost got off at Fiftieth Avenue. He wasn't really intending to. All at once he just found himself standing by the exit door, ready to leave. This was alarming, because Billy Vail had not planned on getting off here. He had never imagined that this was his stop, yet here he was at the door. The sun was beginning to go low in the western sky, and Billy Vail could feel the cool air of evening just outside the door. Behind him his sharp-eyed girl called to him softly, asking him to ride with her a while longer. With great force of will, Billy Vail returned to his seat. Every minute of the bus ride now seemed precious and fleeting.

Thinking about all the landmarks he had wanted to see, and all those he would never see, Billy Vail slowly realized that the excitement was in the ride, and not in the destinations. Still, Billy Vail felt as though he could have—should have—done more, seen more, been more. He supposed all riders felt that way.

Just past Seventieth Avenue, Billy Vail knew his stop was approaching, and a quiet calm fell over him. The rattle and hum of the bus seemed to fade a notch. Billy Vail found himself waiting by the exit door. He could smell the outside air, cool and moist like evening dew on a freshly turned field. The sharp-eyed girl stood beside him, although it was clear that she would not be getting off with him. Billy Vail was happy that she had traveled with him. He realized that it was her trip, too, and he hoped that he had made her happy on the ride. He really wondered about that, and he hoped so. They quietly promised to meet each other on another bus, another trip, fearfully knowing that they could not know what would really happen once they got off the bus.

Out over the western mountaintops, the sun threw one last purple and orange farewell back up into the sky. Billy Vail smiled and stepped off the bus into the night.

All in all, it had been a good trip.

ON A SNOWY EVENING

It took us ten minutes to get the car out of the snowy ditch, but suddenly it rolled free. I didn't know where this mystery girl had come from, but surely she had saved me. I turned to thank her, but she was gone. Squinting in the light of the full moon, I saw the tracks of her narrow boots in the snow, headed off down an overgrown driveway toward a farmhouse I had not noticed before.

Clearly, she had wanted to leave without making a scene, but I had to thank her for helping me.

An old woman met me at the door. I smiled. "A young woman helped me get my car out of the ditch tonight," I said. "Do you have a daughter?"

The old woman shook her head, but as she did, I spotted a picture on the wall in the room behind her.

"That's her," I said. "That's the girl who helped me. Who is she?"

"That's my daughter," the woman said, "but she couldn't have helped you."

I frowned.

"Her car went off the road at the foot of the driveway in a snowstorm." The old woman's eyes blazed. "She's been dead twenty years."

THE WATER'S EDGE

A t the edge of the lake, the killer leaned down, grabbed the tarp firmly in his fists, and pulled the body up over the gunwale into the rowboat. Something heavy thudded against the thwart, and the tarp looked bent at an odd angle, but it was good enough for the short trip to the middle of the lake.

Before loading the heavy rock, the killer looked around carefully. Color drained from the landscape as the sun set out past the wooded horizon. He could smell the muck and mud. A chorus of peepers chirped among the cattails in the marsh to the right. All was quiet and calm.

As he wrestled the rock into the boat, he thought how this had become routine, and as such a bit boring. He wondered if he might improve this part of the plan. Instead of the quick dump-and-run, maybe he could smoke a clove cigarette here at the water's edge, maybe read a poem. Yes, that might bring a little excitement back to the routine.

Then, as he stepped into the boat, a hand rose from the black water and seized his ankle in a bony grip.

FEEDBACK LOOP

Van called me a few minutes after "Rendezvous" went live, and began her critical assessment with three words pronounced with full stops between them: "Oh. My. God."

I took that as a compliment. "You like it?"

"No!" she almost shouted.

This stopped me cold. "Really? I thought it was kind of clever, the way their journeys ended—"

"Oh, I get it," she said. "I understand the story, and don't get me wrong, the writing is very ... nice," she said, though her tone seemed to suggest the opposite.

"If that's the case, then—"

"It's just that ..." She stopped, and I could hear her arranging her thoughts. "Look, I really like your work, and I try to be supportive, but ..." She took a deep breath. "If I find myself in one more story about an ordinary person meeting a strange and unusual way to die, I'll just—" The line went quiet.

"Um," I said tentatively, after a moment. "Funny you should mention that." I forced a chuckle.

No response.

"I'm kind of working on something right now."

No answer.

"Um, Van?"

SILLY PEOPLE

ENEMIES OF THE LIBRARY

A balding man at a folding table of neatly stacked pamphlets spoke to Larry in a kind voice. "Would you like to join the Friends of the Library at the family rate of fifty dollars?"

Larry sucked his breath in through his teeth. "*Friends?* Ooh, that's gonna be a problem."

"We have lower levels of membership, if that would better suit your situation."

"Oh, no, it's not the cost," Larry said. He leaned in and lowered his voice. "The thing is, I already joined the *Enemies* of the Library."

"The Enemies of the Library? What is that?"

"Well, we're a small group. Mostly we get together in the aisles and whisper a little too loudly."

"That doesn't sound so bad."

"And sometimes we borrow books we don't even want to read, just to keep anyone else from reading them."

"Now, that's not very nice."

"And sometimes, we take books down and *reshelve them* instead of putting them on the library carts."

"No! So you're the ones!"

Larry nodded smugly.

The man's face turned an angry red. "Despoilers of civilization."

DANCING FOOL

"I don't care, man. I'm dancing."

"No, now, don't be getting all rash. The sheriff said—"

"I don't give a damn what the sheriff said. I have to listen to my heart. And my heart is telling me to get out there and dance."

"Out where? There ain't no dancin' floor in the whole town. Even when dancin' was legal, nobody wanted to do it."

"That don't matter! I'll dance in the street if I have to. I've just gotsta move my feet!"

"The street?"

"Yeah, man. Dibba-DAH! Dibba-DAH!"

"Hey, don't be doin' that here. I don't need the law on me!"

"You can't stop it! You can't stop it! Look at my feet, man, I'm DANCING!"

"All right, I'm outta here. The way you're acting, won't even need the sheriff. Anybody with any taste at all will come in here and citizens arrest your ass."

"I don't care man. I'm (dibba-DAH!) dancing."

IDEA MAN SANDS THE FLOOR

She stood in the doorway for some time before speaking. Idea Man sat with his back against the white wall, hunched over the project in his lap with a glue gun. Beside him on the floor was a styrofoam bowl of dirty sand he'd scooped out of the gutter in front of the house. Across the room, under the bare windows, the electric hand sander lay where she'd left it yesterday. Though he did not look up from his work, he knew she was frowning, and he felt his own lower lip tighten in response.

"You know," she began hesitantly, "I think if you'd just used the regular sander, you'd be done by now."

"Oh, you'd like that, wouldn't you?" He spoke quietly, but he couldn't keep the bitterness out of his voice. "You'd like me to give up on all my hopes and dreams."

When she spoke again, her voice was even quieter. "I'd just like to get this floor sanded, so we can get the new tile down."

He worked furiously with the glue gun. "That's what I'm doing."

"Um, no," she said, her voice taking on an edge. "You're—" She stopped and cocked her head. "What *are* you doing?"

"I'm inventing," he said. "It's what an inventor does. It's classic."

She stared at him. "What, exactly, are you inventing?"

He put the glue gun down roughly and began to stand up. "They're called 'sanding socks'."

"Sanding socks?"

"Yes! It's a specially designed, reinforced sock with an abrasive surface." He held one up in front of him and stuck his hand inside it to show an uneven patch of sand glued to the bottom. "They're worn like regular socks, but when you walk around the room, you're sanding the floor." He gestured the cracked and gloppy garment at her pointedly. "Sanding socks."

She was still wearing the sanding frown she'd come in with. "Those are just the hiking socks I got you for your birthday, and you're just gluing sand to them with my scrapbook glue gun."

He scoffed. "I'm preparing a uniform abrasive surface," he said. "And I thought your mother said the scrapbooking kit was for *us*."

She looked at him plaintively. "I'll have the curtains and the throw rugs done in a couple hours. Will the floor be sanded, too, so we can get the tile down and the furniture back in here?"

He shrugged and sat down again, now combing through the bowl of sand with his fingertips. "I think so," he said, then added cautiously, "You can't rush an invention, though. You have to let it find its own way into the world."

She stared at him wordlessly for a moment, then she was gone in a swish of ponytail.

Hours later, before she picked up the electric sander and finished the floor herself, she first had to sweep up an unseemly pile of dirty sand, glue stick bits, and twisted sock thread.

Such is life, she thought, when you're married to an idea man.

THE DANGERS OF RABBIT
TOSSING

"It doesn't seem like much of a trick to me," she said

"What? Of course it's a trick. It's a really good trick."

She frowned. "You hold him upside down, and toss him, and he arcs over and lands on his feet." She raised her eyebrows at him. "That's it?"

"What do you mean, 'that's it'?" he said. "It's amazing."

She shook her head a little. "I saw a guy that tossed his cat like that. Cat loved it."

"Well, that's easy," he said indignantly, "because cats always land on their feet. Rabbits don't have natural talent, so it's harder for them to stick the landing." He shrugged. "They bounce around a lot."

"I don't know," she said, her tone turning thoughtful. "Maybe if you added something to it, like maybe you could toss him so he goes through something before he lands."

"Hmm," he said. "I like where you're going with this. Maybe a ring of some kind."

"And maybe," she said, beginning to nod, "it could be on fire."

He brightened. "There's a hula hoop upstairs in the closet!"
"And a can of gas in the garage!"

THE PLUNGER

L arry started up the stairs. He was eager to arrive, eager to grasp the situation and bend it to his own direction. But he did not want to be lulled into complacency by the easy ride of the elevator. No, complacency was a luxury he could not afford, not this mission, not this time.

Arriving at the top of the stairs, he emerged into the warm upstairs hall and headed to the maintenance closet. As he opened the door, his gaze settled on the toilet plunger he had come for, and he let the steely resolve take hold of his brain. He would not—could not—let the situation carry off the way it had last time.

He would not be fooled, as he had before, when he had knocked on the door—intending only to deliver the plunger for the guest to use. That time, the *last* time, when the guest had opened the door, standing there shirtless in his boxer shorts, he had caught Larry off-guard. The guest had stepped back, clearing the way for Larry, and Larry had foolishly taken a single step toward the bathroom. With that step, he was committed. No longer could he simply say "here's the plunger" and be done with the mess. With that single step, he'd committed himself to clearing the toilet blockage.

So foul! Never again. Never!

Standing now in front of the door, his mind set, hand raised to knock, Larry hesitated, suddenly afraid.

☙✦❧

A moment later, Herbert Weiss heard a knock on his hotel door. Good heavens, he thought, I hope that's the maintenance man.

Opening the door, he was surprised to find a toilet plunger standing in the doorway, alone, still wobbling a little on its rubber base. On down the hallway, a bald-headed man was leaving in a hurry. As the bald man reached the doorway to the stairs, Herbert heard him shout back over his shoulder, "Plunger's in the hall for you. Have a good night!"

And then he was gone, the pneumatic arm closing the stairway door behind him.

What a strange person, thought Herbert.

CUTE RABBIT STORY

They found the rabbit dead when they got home from school, and dragged me out to the hutch a few minutes later. Short Kid poked at the stiff body with a stick through the open access door.

I nodded and sucked my breath in sadly. "Yep," I said, "that sucker's dead."

"What?" said Tall Kid in a frantic voice. "How?"

"Well, look at these." I pointed at the snow, where dirty paw prints circled the hutch like a crazy hula hoop. "Some stray dogs must have chased him around the pen until his heart gave out."

"Why would they do that?" Tall Kid asked, struggling to hold back tears. "We've had him since he was this big." She held out a cupped hand.

I shrugged. "They're *dogs*. It's what they do."

The dam broke, and Tall Kid ran to the house in a flood of tears.

Short Kid studied me seriously. "All rabbits go to heaven, right?" he asked.

I shook my head. "No, you're thinking of dogs."

He frowned. "Well, where do rabbits go?"

I looked at the snow. "If the ground isn't too frozen," I said, "down about two feet."

IDEA MAN FIXES THE WASHER

I dea Man had a lot of work to do, so he started at dawn. Well, not *exactly* dawn. He was tired, he worked *hard* for a living. "What?" he asked her. "You think it's easy coming up with good ideas all the time?"

Anyway, he got started about nine. At least, that's when he started his coffee and turned on the news. He was thinking about the job, though, so he counted it as starting. "You can't do a job unless you've thought it through first," he told her.

When she left at a little before noon, he jumped up to get busy. She wouldn't understand if he was still in front of the television when she left. She didn't know how the inventing mind worked. Even while he was hauling out the tools, though, she found a way to nag him. "I *know* I'm still in my underwear," he said. "It doesn't make any sense to take a shower and put on clean clothes when I'm just about to dive into a big job and get really dirty."

While she was at the store, he really got things done. Though the space was tight in the laundry room, everything came apart just like he'd planned it. He felt tremendous clarity and focus, and he didn't even take a break the whole time she was gone. Did this make her happy? No. When she returned nearly three hours later, all she did was complain.

She stood in the doorway of the laundry room, a nasty look on her face. "What are you doing?" she asked.

He looked down at the parts strewn about the room. He'd tried to keep things organized as he took it apart, but it had gotten a little out of hand. Who knew a washing machine had so many parts? "I have to take it apart if you want me to fix it," he said.

She looked at him, frowned, and blinked. "It's the dryer that's broken."

A WINNING NAME

"Hey, man, I just wanted to tell you I thought of a name."

"A name? What for? You get a dog?"

"No, for me."

"You already have a name."

"My dance name, you know."

"*Dance name?*"

"Yeah. All the famous dancers have names."

"Um, yeah, their own names."

"Freddy Two Shoes."

"Freddy Two Shoes?"

"*Freddy Two Shoes!*"

"Um. I don't know how to tell you this—wait, yes I do. That's the dumbest thing I ever heard."

"No, way, man. It's got rhythm, like me."

"It's like you because it's dumb. For one thing, everybody's got two shoes."

"Not everybody. Some people out there only have one foot, and some people don't have any."

"Those people aren't dancers."

"But I'm a dancer, and I've got two shoes."

"And, your name is not Fred. It's Jim."

"So, what? I'm telling you it's a great dance name. It's a winning name."

"And I'm telling you it's stupid."

"I'm going to use it. You'll see."

"I can't believe I even talk to you."

Six months later, the tri-county, all-ages tap contest was won ... by Freddy Two Shoes.

LARRY HARRISON'S NIGHT SHIFT

A t three minutes before eleven, Larry threw open the lobby doors and entered the hotel like a conquering hero. It was Thursday night. It was his first night back to work after his regular two days off. And it was great to be here.

Larry loved his job.

He was wearing the required pressed white shirt, the uniform tie, and a big smile. He'd given up wearing the beret, and he was sure his bald head was gleaming in the lobby lights, but he no longer cared. One of his thin hands held a coffee mug, the other a leather organizer.

He surveyed the lobby quickly. The plants, the over-stuffed couches in front of the television armoire, the coffee stand at the corner of the breakfast dining area, all were in order. The tile floor shone in the fluorescent lamps. The air smelled of commercial cleansers. Everything was perfect for a cozy, respectable, thriving, mysterious, cosmic and microcosmic hotel.

"Good morning, Louise," he said brightly to the twenty-ish girl behind the front desk, "right on time." Saying it was morning when it was actually night was a very old joke, but one he never tired of.

She scowled at him. She had her sweater on and purse in her hand and her notebook under her arm and she was ready to go. "I haven't seen anything good about it," she stated flatly.

He cheerfully ignored her and stopped by the coffee machine in the breakfast area to fill up his mug. By the time his mug was full, she was out the door and into the night, the glass door closing behind her.

She hadn't stayed while he counted the drawer, but he understood that. He'd occasionally worked the afternoon shift —her shift, three to eleven—and it always seemed to drag by. She liked working here, but she didn't love her job the way he loved his. When he came in, she was ready to go home. If he couldn't arrive a few minutes early to count the cash in the register—and he almost never could—he had no right to expect her to stay late. Absolutely understandable.

All the same, he wondered what she was hiding.

He didn't have a chance to wonder for long, though. He had just gone behind the front desk when the first guest of the evening walked in. She was an elderly woman, dressed in a shabby floral-print sun dress. The front door closed behind her as she walked carefully across the tile into the lobby.

As he watched her, he wondered idly what she would think if a hooker walked in.

He sized her up quickly. She wasn't coming straight to the front desk; instead, she made her way around the lobby slowly, appraising the hotel even as he appraised her. She didn't have reservations, because if she did it would have been too late to cancel them, but she had come for a room. From the satisfied look on her face, she was happy with the quality. She was by herself, most likely, because old women rarely get sent into the lobby alone to get the room if they have company. She finished her assessment of the coffee station—and he could tell from the look on her face that she'd be down in the morning for coffee— and came over to the front desk at last.

"How much is a room?" she asked, her voice gentle. She reminded him of his grandmother.

"For how many people?" he returned, though he already knew what she would say.

"Just one," she said sweetly.

Larry smiled, thoroughly pleased with his ability to read people. Just about everyone checking into the hotel wanted a room for one, no matter how many people there really were. This was one of the few times he believed that. He told her the price, including the generous senior discount, and she said that would be fine.

"Do you have something downstairs?" she asked. He'd known she would ask that, too.

Larry frowned at the rack, where the registration cards and reservation slips occupied slots representing rooms. He hadn't verified the board yet, but it showed all the downstairs rooms as occupied. A single reservation slip still held a downstairs room. He pulled it out and looked at it. The name on the reservation was Ferringer, and it was for a downstairs room, and it was guaranteed, meaning the guest had guaranteed he would pay for the room and the hotel had guaranteed it would hold it for him. He looked at the clock. What were the chances Ferringer was still coming in? If Ferringer didn't show up, he wouldn't miss his downstairs room. On the other hand ...

Larry pulled the reservation out of the slot for room 114 and put it in a slot upstairs. "I think I can give you this down-stairs room," he said, flashing the old woman a big smile of straight, white, teeth. She smiled back, though not, he noticed, as big or as white. She seemed sweet, though. She really did remind him of his grandmother. "It has two beds," Larry continued, "but I won't charge you extra for that."

"Thank you," said the old woman. "You're a very nice young man."

As she filled out the registration card, Larry started organizing his shift. By the time she was finished, he had counted the drawer. As she headed off to her room, he inventoried and organized the previous shifts' paperwork. He freshened the night coffee, checked the remaining reservations, double-checked the down rooms, verified the occupied rooms on the rack, and balanced the credit cards, still finding time to check in the occasional guest.

When he finally felt he was on top of the shift, he glanced up at the clock. It was almost one a.m. He inhaled deeply, slowly, sensing that the challenge was about to begin.

❦

It started, like it did so many times, with the phone ringing.

"Front desk," Larry said, full of enthusiasm. The phone showed him that the call was coming from room 232, in the back. As a habit, he pulled the registration card for the room, to get an idea about who he was talking to, and what he should be hearing. This room was registered to one person, a truck driver.

"This is room 232. Can I get a six a.m. wake-up call?" asked a dainty voice, certainly not a truck driver named Chuck.

"You sure can," he said slowly, smiling grimly to himself while punching buttons, "and you're all set."

"Thanks, bye."

Larry made a quick note on the card that there were probably two people in the room and replaced the card in the rack.

"Front desk, this is security," sounded the radio. It was Douglas Dent, the security guard.

Larry picked the radio up from its cradle on the back counter and keyed the mic. "Go ahead, Doug," he said.

"Those people in room 215—are they supposed to have a dog?"

"Let me check," Larry said, and paused for a minute, staring at the ceiling, pretending to check. This, too, was an old joke. "Nope," he said finally. "The sign still says 'No Pets'."

"Well, they're walking their dog by the bushes in the parking lot right now," Doug said.

"Fine," Larry said. "Let me know when they return to their room."

"Right."

The phone was ringing again, this time room 335. "Front desk," Larry said, still cheerful.

"Hi," said the man on the phone. "We're in room 335 ..." They always said what room they were in, though for decades hotel phone systems have told the front desk this information automatically. "... and we were wondering if we could get some extra towels."

"Sure," said Larry. The registration card told him the room was rented to two adults and two children. "How many do you need?"

"I think ten oughtta do," he said.

"Hmm," Larry said, feigning thought. There were already enough towels in the room for two adults and two kids. Larry didn't mind giving out extra towels, but he certainly couldn't give ten towels to every room that asked. "I don't think I have that many down here," he lied casually. He pretended to look around, opening a cupboard door and slamming it for effect. Guests always wanted lots of extra towels. The hotel, of course, kept track of the towels given out, as well as the towels that didn't come back. The housekeeping staff would be very unhappy if Larry gave away ten towels that went out in the guest's luggage. "Will four do?"

"I guess so," the guest said.

"I'll have them brought right up."

Larry hung up the phone, replaced the registration card, and took four bath towels off the big stack under the back counter. Picking up the radio, he hailed the security guard.

"Go ahead," said Doug.

"I need you to come down to the front desk for a moment," Larry said. "I need you to take some towels up to a room."

There was a long pause. "Okay," came the response finally.

Immediately, the phone rang again. Room 303 this time.

"Front desk," said Larry, still cheerful.

"Uh, yeah," said what sounded like a teenage girl. Surprisingly, this room was actually registered to two people. Two local people. Eighty percent of the trouble at the hotel came from twenty percent of the guests: the local people. "Can we get an ashtray in room 228?"

"Uh, no," Larry said. "You're in a non-smoking room."

"Uh, we asked for a *smoking* room," she said, then turned to say something he couldn't catch to the other person in the room, then, "Why did you do that?" Then, to Larry, "Never *mind*." And hung up.

The elevator door slid open and Douglas Dent walked into the lobby, his security uniform all shiny and pressed. Doug's face was downcast and sour as he trudged up to the front desk. "You know," he said, "it's really hard to be effective security when I have to be delivering towels and pillows all the time. I can't be watching the parking lot when I'm traipsing up the stairs with a load of towels." He paused to sigh heavily. "I can't watch what's going on in the back when I'm always making deliveries."

Larry smiled sympathetically and nodded. "I know," he

said, with what could have passed for compassion in his voice. He slid the four towels across the counter to Doug. "I need you to take these towels up to room 335," he said.

Sighing heavily again for effect, Doug scooped the towels off the counter, turned, and headed back to the elevator.

"Did the people with the dog go back to their room?" Larry asked after him.

"I think so," said Doug back over his shoulder. "But I couldn't tell for sure because I was playing delivery boy."

"Fine," said Larry. He picked up the phone and dialed 215. The registration card said they were from out of state, and here for only one night.

The man in the room answered the phone on one ring.

"Uh," said Larry. "We've been advised that you have a dog," he said. Larry hated making these calls. "And I'm required to remind you that the hotel does not allow pets."

"Oh, we don't have a dog," the man lied pleasantly.

This did not surprise Larry. "No dog, then?" he asked.

"Nope," said the man.

"Okay," said Larry. "Well, have a good night, then." As they hung up, he made a note on the card to *not* re-rent to those people.

Right then the lobby door opened, and a little Italian-looking man entered and walked up to the front desk. He had his black hair slicked back and was dressed wearing a tan suit and gold chains, like he had been out on a date or to a dancing club, and he smelled like expensive cologne. "How much is a room?" he asked.

"For how many people?" asked Larry, though he knew the answer already. This was a local person, not a traveler. He had been out at a club, and there was no way he had come to a hotel to be alone. Larry had not seen him drive up because he had not, in fact, driven up. He had parked away from the front door, so he was likely hiding the passenger in his car. And he was, of course, going to give the stock answer.

"Just one," said the little man, noticeably averting his eyes.

"Of course," said Larry, and quoted him the price for two people.

The man took his wallet from his back pocket and looked at his money, then said that would be all right. When Larry asked him for his identification, he saw that the man had an address only a couple miles from the hotel.

Later, when he saw the guest heading to his room with a female companion, Larry was not surprised.

Douglas Dent was on the radio again, "Front desk, this is security," he said.

"Go ahead, Doug," said Larry.

"The people in 313, are they supposed to have a pet?"

Larry paused, running his fingers absently over his bald head and sighing at the floor. "Still no," he said finally into the microphone.

"Well," said Doug, "they have a cat sitting in their window."

The frenetic pace of phone and radio and guests continued like that for ninety long minutes—towels here, roll-a-way there, wake-up call here, pizza delivery number there, crib here, do you cash third-party checks (*no*) there, cat here, dog there—

By the time the night fell quiet, about two a.m., Larry felt out of breath.

The elevator chimed, the doors slid open, and Doug, who had completely used up his supply of heavy sighs, walked into the lobby.

"Did you see that old woman?" he asked Larry. "She checked into room 112 right about eleven o'clock?"

"What about her?" asked Larry, suddenly feeling nauseous.

"She's got a whole carload of people with her. Looked like four or five adults and at least four kids. I don't suppose she claimed all those people when she checked in?"

Now it was Larry's turn to sigh deeply. "No," he said dejectedly. The old woman, the woman who reminded him of his grandmother, the one person he had trusted the whole night, had lied to him. "I'll make a note of it on the card," he said. "I'm too tired to deal with it tonight."

As he was making the note on the registration card, headlights played across the lobby doors and windows. A car pulled up and parked right in front of the door. The driver got out slowly, stretched, and came in. "Hello," he said. "I should have a reservation for a downstairs room here. My name is Ferringer."

"Ah, yes," said Larry. "I should have expected you right about now." To himself, under his breath, he muttered, "*Every night!*"

COMPENSATION

Next to last, here's an item that is not a short story but instead a one-act play I wrote in the time of the rest of these stories. I always had designs on making this into a short story, but I think it works well—and is hilarious—just the way it is. Enjoy!

CHARACTERS

GENERAL RICHARDS: An army general excited about his plan

COLONEL JOHNSON: Logistics officer, very high voice, eager to please

COLONEL PAIN: Operations officer who doesn't like the plan

SETTING

A military planning room near the front of a war.

ACTION

GENERAL RICHARDS stands alone in a military planning room, looking down at a map on a table.

GENERAL RICHARDS: Johnson! Pain! Get in here!

COLONEL JOHNSON enters at a trot. COLONEL PAIN enters more hesitantly.

COLONEL JOHNSON: Yes, sir!

GENERAL RICHARDS: I want a full report about how Operation Soft Talk is going.

COLONEL PAIN and COLONEL JOHNSON look warily at each other.

COLONEL JOHNSON: It's not quite a success, yet, sir.

COLONEL PAIN: That's putting it mildly.

GENERAL RICHARDS: What do you mean?

COLONEL JOHNSON: We're a bit weak to the south, sir—

COLONEL PAIN: We're being completely overrun all along our southern flank.

GENERAL RICHARDS: What?!

COLONEL PAIN: The second and third battalions have both lost a lot of men, as well as a lot of ground, sir.

GENERAL RICHARDS turns to COLONEL JOHNSON.

GENERAL RICHARDS: Is this true?

COLONEL JOHNSON looks at the floor.

COLONEL JOHNSON: It's true, sir.

GENERAL RICHARDS: Has my secret weapon been deployed as I instructed?

COLONEL JOHNSON: *Exactly* as you instructed, sir.

COLONEL PAIN: To the letter.

GENERAL RICHARDS: You put enough men into the fabrication effort to create the number of the weapons that I specified?

COLONEL JOHNSON: Yes, sir.

GENERAL RICHARDS: And you diverted the attack helicopters to drop the weapon as I put down in the plan?

COLONEL JOHNSON: Yes, sir.

GENERAL RICHARDS: And it hasn't had *any* effect?

COLONEL PAIN (dryly): I wouldn't say that, sir. It *has* cost us a lot of men.

GENERAL RICHARDS: That can't be!

GENERAL RICHARDS paces thoughtfully for a second.

GENERAL RICHARDS: I'm going to get a current situation report from the battalion commanders. I'll be right back. You two stay here.

GENERAL RICHARDS exits.

COLONEL PAIN: Listen, we have to do something about this.

COLONEL JOHNSON: About what?

COLONEL PAIN: About General Richards' so-called *plan*. We have to talk him out of it.

COLONEL JOHNSON: Why?

COLONEL PAIN: *Why?* How about because it doesn't make any sense? How about because the whole thing is *idiotic!*

COLONEL JOHNSON: No, I wouldn't say that. I think it has some good points that we can build on—

COLONEL PAIN: Listen. The *reality* of the situation is that we are fighting a war, and we have to make a plan that will connect to the *reality* of fighting a war. General Richards' plan doesn't even *begin* to connect to that reality.

COLONEL JOHNSON: Well, a lot of people would disagree with you about that. His plan is based on some really good ideas that a lot of other people support.

COLONEL PAIN: We can't fight a war with good ideas if they don't connect with reality.

GENERAL RICHARDS enters, looking grim.

GENERAL RICHARDS: Well, it's true, we're being overrun in the south. You know what this means?

COLONEL PAIN: Yes, I do, sir. It means—

GENERAL RICHARDS: It *means* we have to redouble the effort of Operation Soft Talk right away!

COLONEL JOHNSON: Right away, sir!

GENERAL RICHARDS: We're going to need to put more men into the fabrication effort. I want you to pull another company of men off the line and get them working on my weapon.

COLONEL JOHNSON: Right, sir!

GENERAL RICHARDS: We're going to need to divert more helicopters away from the bombing and support roles, get them to work dropping the weapon.

COLONEL JOHNSON: Right, sir!

GENERAL RICHARDS (thoughtfully): Maybe we can remove the guns from the helicopters, make more room for my special weapon.

COLONEL PAIN: No, no, no!

GENERAL RICHARDS: What?

COLONEL PAIN: I think we have to try another plan, sir.

GENERAL RICHARDS looks very unhappy.

COLONEL JOHNSON: I think what Colonel Pain means, sir, is that the plan for Operation Soft Talk has a lot of good points, but maybe we just need to tweak it a little.

COLONEL PAIN: No, no, no! I'm saying we need to try a completely different approach. A direct assault with *real* weapons.

GENERAL RICHARDS: Are you saying that you don't understand the weapons of Operation Soft Talk?

COLONEL PAIN: Weapons? *Weapons?*

COLONEL PAIN reaches down to the table and holds up a rectangular package.

COLONEL PAIN: Sir, an oversize condom is not a proper weapon of war!

GENERAL RICHARDS: You watch your tone, Colonel, or I'll have you brought up on charges of insubordination.

COLONEL PAIN: Sir, our men are trained to fight. We should develop a plan that lets them fight—

GENERAL RICHARDS: You listen to me. I've been an officer in this man's army for twenty-seven years, and I've forgotten more than you'll ever know about good combat plans.

COLONEL PAIN: How do you see this as a good plan for *combat?*

GENERAL RICHARDS: You've got a lot to learn about psychological operations.

COLONEL PAIN: With all due respect, *sir*, I'm highly trained and experienced in psychological operations—

GENERAL RICHARDS: Well, you clearly don't understand what's going on here.

COLONEL PAIN: Oh, I think I do, sir.

GENERAL RICHARDS takes the oversize condom from COLONEL PAIN and holds it up admiringly.

GENERAL RICHARDS: The enemy puts a lot of stock in penis size, Colonel. When they see these condoms, and they think they're our regular condoms, they'll be too intimidated to fight. They'll surrender in droves.

COLONEL PAIN: I understand the concept, sir—

GENERAL RICHARDS: Well, it doesn't seem that you do.

COLONEL PAIN: If your plan is so good, sir, then why isn't it working?

GENERAL RICHARDS: It isn't working, *Colonel*, because I'm constantly being undermined by people who don't know how to fight a war!

COLONEL JOHNSON: We need more respect for the chain of command!

GENERAL RICHARDS: Exactly. Now, Colonel Johnson, I need you to get those extra drums of latex and sawed-off baseball bats to the fabrication area right away.

COLONEL JOHNSON: Right away, sir.

GENERAL RICHARDS: Colonel Pain, I need you to get more troops to the fabrication effort.

COLONEL PAIN: You want me to take *more* troops *away* from the battle, to make *condoms*?

GENERAL RICHARDS: Right. And pull back some more of the attack helicopters. We need a lot more air support to get these things into the battle.

COLONEL PAIN: Sir, I really believe that we should develop a plan to let our men fight like they know how to fight. Get them to the front, get them ammunition and air support, and stay out of their way.

GENERAL RICHARDS stops his activity and slowly turns to COLONEL PAIN.

GENERAL RICHARDS: You still don't see the method to my madness?

COLONEL PAIN: I don't see ... any method ... at all, sir.

GENERAL RICHARDS is disappointed and so angry as to be shaking.

GENERAL RICHARDS: Go and get me the latest situation reports.

COLONEL PAIN opens his mouth to speak, slowly changes his mind, turns, and exits.

GENERAL RICHARDS: Forget him. If he doesn't see the light by now he's an idiot anyway.

COLONEL JOHNSON: He should learn to trust the judgment of his superior officers.

GENERAL RICHARDS: Now, we're going to need a lot more latex. Have you got those reserves I ordered up yet?

COLONEL JOHNSON: It's standing by, sir.

GENERAL RICHARDS turns thoughtful.

GENERAL RICHARDS: Perhaps it would help some if we made them ... bigger.

COLONEL JOHNSON: Whatever you say, sir.

COLONEL PAIN enters carrying a paper and looking grim.

COLONEL PAIN: Well, it's over.

GENERAL RICHARDS: What?

COLONEL PAIN holds up the paper as evidence.

COLONEL PAIN: We just got a message from Washington. The President's ordering a complete withdrawal. The war is over.

GENERAL RICHARDS grabs the paper and studies it.

GENERAL RICHARDS: That can't be!

COLONEL JOHNSON: We were so close to winning! General Richards' plan was *bound* to work!

COLONEL PAIN: *Bound to work?* We had the chance to really *do* something, to attack, to use the skills and training of our soldiers to really *fight*—

GENERAL RICHARDS: You listen! I've been a commander in this man's army for twenty-seven years—

COLONEL PAIN: Yes, yes, we've all heard, twenty-seven years. And what has all that experience done for us?

COLONEL PAIN picks up one of the oversized condoms.

COLONEL PAIN: All your so-called *wisdom* has gotten us is defeat, and a bunch of condoms that won't even *fit* anybody but *me*.

COLONEL PAIN exits dejectedly. GENERAL RICHARDS and COLONEL JOHNSON are silent for a moment.

COLONEL JOHNSON: That was insubordination if I ever saw it.

GENERAL RICHARDS: He obviously doesn't understand psychological operations.

COLONEL JOHNSON: He should be more receptive to the experience of his superior officers.

GENERAL RICHARDS: He damn well should. But forget him for now. I'll make sure his next post is commanding latrine detail in Alaska.

COLONEL JOHNSON: It's better than he deserves.

GENERAL RICHARDS: Now, about this withdrawal. I'm sure it's just a temporary tactic to confuse the enemy. We'll modify the plans to leave the condoms behind as we withdraw, and when we return, the enemy will be too afraid of us to pick up a rifle.

COLONEL JOHNSON: Right, sir. We'll just modify the plans slightly to compensate for the withdrawal.

GENERAL RICHARDS: That's right. It's just a little matter of compensation.

THE STORY OF THE BOOK

F irst there was The Book. It was a great book, hailed as a new classic by critics and readers alike. It had no demographic, but was meant for all of mankind, a masterpiece for the ages.

Then came the movie, targeted at the primary movie-going demographic of 18- to 35-year-olds. Fans of The Book complained that the themes had been dumbed down.

Next came the book based on the movie, targeted at young adult readers. Fans of the movie complained that the book failed to capture the sweeping grandeur of the film.

Then came the television series, targeted at Generation Now, based on the book based on the movie. Nobody liked it.

Then came the cartoon series, simplified from the television series and targeted at the Saturday-morning demographic of tweens.

Along the way, there were playing cards, a video game, and a breakfast cereal, carefully carving up the market of movie tie-ins.

In the end, there was The Book, gutted of potential, known

by all, dismissed by most, and treasured by the few who actually read it.

ABOUT THE AUTHOR

Born and raised in upstate New York, Terry F. Torrey has spent most of his adult life in Arizona with his amazing wife, awesome daughter, and remarkable cats. A lifelong learner, he was most pleased to complete the acclaimed Creative Writing program at Phoenix College.

Terry F. Torrey writes an eclectic variety of quirky, compelling, and heartfelt books and shorts, including campy but realistic pop-culture monster novels, page-turning vigilante action novels, riveting suspense novels with shades of noir, cozy upstate campus mysteries, clean contemporary westerns, and sharp works of political satire.

Find all of Terry F. Torrey's writings at terryftorrey.com.

www.ingramcontent.com/pod-product-compliance
Lightning Source LLC
Chambersburg PA
CBHW051952170626
46808CB00007B/2583